Buzzing Easter Bunnies

Every story needs a decent climax...

There are plenty of things Christina Barclay would like to do before she hits thirty at Easter. Having an orgasm with somebody else in the room is most definitely one of them.

Up to now, her love life has been sorely lacking in the toe-curling department - but luckily for Christina, she's just started dating Matthew Adrian Bunion, a man whose bedroom inexperience is more than made up for by his never-ending enthusiasm. Mr Bunion will not rest until his new girlfriend is satisfied - no matter what the cost in rechargeable batteries, physical injury or public embarrassment.

From the best-selling author of *BLUE CHRISTMAS BALLS* and *LOVE... FROM BOTH SIDES*, this is the story of one woman and one man on an epic quest to come together, and celebrate an Easter birthday in style.

By Nick Spalding:

Love... From Both Sides
Love... And Sleepless Nights
Love... Under Different Skies

Life… With No Breaks
Life… On A High

Blue Christmas Balls
Buzzing Easter Bunnies

Max Bloom In... The Cornerstone
Wordsmith... The Cornerstone Book 2

Spalding's Scary Shorts

Buzzing Easter Bunnies

Nick Spalding

CHRISTINA

I *will* have an orgasm this year.
As God is my witness, I bloody well *will*.

...with a man, I mean. I will have an orgasm with an *actual live man* for the first time in my life, or my name isn't Christina Hayley Enid Barclay.

I've been climaxing successfully on my own since the age of fourteen of course, but then I know what I'm doing down there, don't I?

The same cannot be said for the men I have been involved with my whole life.

Sadly, every time I have set alight to all of my nerve endings, it's been because I have fast, dextrous fingers, and the ability to imagine all sorts of interesting scenarios involving me, Gerard Butler, some flimsy clothing, and a super king sized bed.

Not once has it happened with a real, live penis in the room.

It is a sorry, sorry state of affairs, I'm sure you'll agree (not that I don't enjoy fantasising about Mr Butler, you understand).

Luckily, I think I've finally met a man who can help me with my problem, even if he is going to need a bit of, er, *training*.

I've never dated a virgin before, but I think I may have struck gold with young Matt Bunion anyway. He is kind, thoughtful, funny - and most importantly - *eager to please.*

It never occurred to me that an inexperienced man could be my best bet for sexual gratification, to tell the truth. Until now I've spent my life looking for Mr Right among men who have - by and large - been there, done that and sold the t-shirt on eBay for a fiver.

And that's where I've been going wrong. Experienced men - in *my* experience - always turn out to be complete arseholes, for one reason or another. They tend to think they're God's gift to humanity, despite all evidence to the contrary.

It seems that once the owner of a penis has sown his wild oats a few times, he becomes convinced that he is an expert at relationships; as if having sex with half a dozen women means you gain complete insight into the minds of the other three billion walking the planet.

Each and every time I think I'm on to a winner, I end up being disappointed. Disappointment is not an emotional state conducive to soaring orgasms, I think you'll agree - hence my problem.

While I've always been concerned about my inability to achieve a satisfying climax when there is a penis involved, it's only been in the past few months that the issue has really started to play on my mind. My thirtieth birthday is rapidly approaching on Easter Sunday, and not reaching a proper climax with a man before the end of your twenties just isn't normal. Even if a majority of the men I've dated have been disappointing, at least one of them should have been able to do the deed, surely? To supply me with the correct instruments and expertise, so to speak?

This train of thought leads me to a rather disturbing conclusion. It might not be them. It might be *me*.

Even if Gerard Butler did knock on my door dressed as a half naked Spartan warrior, offering me a night of sexual congress with his washboard stomach and glistening muscles, there's a disturbing possibility that I wouldn't be able to have an orgasm, no matter what he did with his tongue, fingers, and Gerard Butler Junior.

This is a worrying concept. A *very* worrying concept, indeed.

So, this is the quandary I find myself in. On the one hand, I have had a series of unsatisfying relationships with men I should have avoided like the plague, but on the other, there's every chance I have a clitoris more temperamental than the twenty quid hair straighteners I bought at the market last year.

Here's an idea: let me describe a few of my previous sexual experiences, and you can decide for me.

I don't think there's much point in dwelling on what happened with Pete Cavendish though. The poor chap was obviously in complete denial of his rampant homosexuality at the time, and you don't really want to read several paragraphs detailing his attempts to insert his flaccid member into me. Just picture pushing a strand of cooked spaghetti through a tea strainer and you'll get the general idea.

In no particular order then:

1. Darren Malloy.

I met Darren clubbing one night back when that kind of thing appealed to me. No stranger to Lacoste polo shirts and espadrilles, Darren was the kind of man your mother would probably have warned you about, if he wasn't so slippery.

My relationship with Darren lasted five months, most of which were spent watching him get ready in front of the mirror, and listening to his boring anecdotes about the work he'd done on his Vauxhall Nova that week. If the boy had spent as much time on my clitoris as he did on his exhaust, my problems would have been over before they'd begun.

As it was, Darren was pretty good in bed, but in the twenty or thirty times we had sex, I never once came close to climaxing. He had a decent sized penis and knew what to do with it after a fashion, but I think I was permanently put off by the gold necklace he insisted on wearing twenty four-seven. It would invariably smack me on the bridge of the nose every time he was on top and thrusting his way to ejaculation. And that bugger was heavy, let me tell you (the necklace, not Darren). Some women complain that after rough sex they suffer from bruised thighs. I should've been so lucky. You could tell how much of a good time Darren had had with me, just by the amount of foundation I had to apply the next day to cover up the swelling between my eyes.

2. Doctor Adil Hannan.

When you're a freshly minted nurse in your first three months on the wards, there's nothing sexier than a young, fit and handsome doctor smiling warmly at you as he passes by in the corridor outside the x-ray department. Adil was a gorgeous Indian, with a set of the most striking brown eyes I've ever... well, laid eyes on. He was intelligent, softly spoken with a light Indian lilt, and unfailingly pleasant to be around. Unfortunately Adil also had a worrying tendency to talk dirty during sex.

This was surprising and a bit disconcerting in and of itself, given that in company, Adil would never swear, hardly ever raise his voice, and was the most even tempered person I've ever come across. Hearing filth spew from his lips during intercourse made it feel like you were having sex with Mumbai's answer to Dr Jekyll and Mr Hyde. However, I'm not averse to a bit of dirty talk. In the right circumstances, and delivered in the correct manner, it can be breathlessly exciting. Adil didn't really get it though. I don't know if it was because he was a doctor or not, but his idea of dirty talk was extremely *clinical*.

'Oh Christina,' he would whisper into my ear. 'I'm going to insert my penis so deep into your engorged vagina that your nerve endings will be on fire.' *Wow.* How can a girl not get excited hearing those words? 'Oh Christina,' he would continue. 'Would you slide the middle digit of your hand into my rectum, find my prostate and massage it for me please?'

I'm fairly sure those exact same words can be found in the last medical text book I read about conducting prostate exams in men over the age of fifty.

My relationship with Adil lasted just three months. I can't say it was one that uplifted my soul in any way, but it did improve my knowledge of sexual biology no end. It was an area I hadn't paid enough attention to in college, so I was glad of the refresher.

Needless to say, Adil's scientific approach to bedtime shenanigans did nothing to increase my chances of having an orgasm. Or, as Adil liked to put it: 'the sudden discharge of accumulated sexual tension, resulting in rhythmic muscular contractions caused by sexual pleasure.'

How are you supposed to cum your brains out when the man you're with uses the word *discharge* in relation to it?

4. Simon Addison

Simon Addison remains the nicest man I've ever had a relationship with.

My God he was *nice*.

He had nice features, nice manners, a nice voice, a nice car, a nice flat, and a nice penis.

We'd do *nice* things together, like go for long walks in nice places, eat in nice restaurants, and see nice movies at the cinema.

We also had nice sex.

Nice, nice, nice, nice, *nice*.

I was more likely to have an orgasm watching my underwear going round in the tumble dryer than I was in bed with Simon Addison.

The relationship with him lasted six months... somehow. Then one morning he produced a packet of Nice biscuits to dunk in our tea and I lost my mind.

About a year after I broke up with him, a friend of a friend told me that Simon had just been arrested for drug trafficking. I wasn't surprised in the slightest. No-one can be that bloody *nice* without hiding something.

4. 'Big Rob' Pottinger

Ah, you can picture him already, can't you? Any man with a name like 'Big Rob' has to look a certain way, doesn't he? Over six feet tall, shoulders like a bull, able to drink his own bodyweight in lager without passing out...

All these things were true of Big Rob Pottinger. Being in a relationship with him was rather like owning an extremely large dog. Fun to be around, but you're never entirely sure that you're completely safe. One minute you could be having a whale of a time, the next you could be flat on your back, having been accidentally knocked over by the big lumbering sod.

This was the kind of man who could attend a wedding wearing a kilt (even though he was about as Scottish as spaghetti bolognaise) and pull it off with absolutely no trouble at all. That's how big and looming he was. There were times I considered buying crampons and a thick rope just so I could get up there to give him a proper kiss.

Big Rob was big in every department. Enormous, in fact. *Worryingly* large. The first time I saw it I nearly had a heart attack. My cervix started to ache just at the prospect of it.

But Big Rob - much like his big, dumb dog equivalent - was surprisingly gentle. He was obviously aware of how prodigious his member was, and was therefore at pains to make sure *I* didn't feel any pain myself. It still felt like giving birth in reverse though. Rob had to conduct extensive and complicated foreplay in order to get me into a fit state to receive his sizeable contribution, and even then we had to go very, *very* slowly. Of course this meant that achieving an orgasm was difficult for him, and entirely impossible for me. He couldn't get past walking pace, and I was too concerned with the state of my internal workings to give any thought to reaching a climax. Most of the time I'd end up using my right hand on him, while trying to sit in as comfortable a position as possible. I seriously have no idea how the girls in porno movies do it. If I had to swap places with one of them, the movie would have to be called 'Two Seconds Of Hardcore Sex And A Trip To Casualty'.

I bumped into Big Rob and his new wife a few months ago in Asda. She seemed like a very nice girl - and certainly looked more robust than me. I swear I detected a noticeable limp as she walked away on her husband's arm though.

5. Cock Features.

His name wasn't actually Cock Features, but Steven Bradley was such a tosser of the highest order that I cannot bring myself to refer to him by his real name.

Cock Features was my first long term boyfriend. I met him when I was nineteen and he was twenty five. At the time I was deliriously happy to be dating a man that much older than myself. These days I realise that the only practical upshot of him being six years older than me, was that it had given him an extra half decade or so to really master the art of manipulating younger women.

And *boy* was I manipulated. Both mentally and physically.

Cock Features would feed me bullshit about love, commitment and caring - while shagging another girl at the same time. He was presumably feeding her all the same lines he fed me, and judging by the fact he kept the charade up for nearly a year, she must have been as taken in by it as I was.

It didn't help that Cock Features was almost unnaturally good looking. A combination of the lead singer from A-ha and Orlando Bloom, he had that whole 'fey' thing going on that at the time, I thought was just about the sexiest thing ever.

As a young and inexperienced woman, rugged manly types terrified me, so to have the attention of an androgynous, non-threatening man like Cock Features was an apparent blessing. He was charming, interesting and attentive. He was also the most self-centered human being who has ever walked the face of the planet, so it should come as absolutely no surprise that he was awful in bed.

He didn't actually ever have sex with me. It was more like he used me as something convenient to masturbate into. The sex (such as it was) only ever lasted as long as he wanted it to. He would invariably climax as quickly as possible, before issuing a perfunctory kiss and a hoarsely whispered lie. 'Thanks baby. I love you,' he'd say, before rolling over and turning on the TV without so much as another glance in my direction.

My blood still boils when I think about the oily little prick, even a decade later.

Being nineteen, and not knowing any better, I tolerated that shit for *months*. You can imagine how much damage a relationship like that can do to your self esteem. Being treated like an ambulatory blow-up sex doll is a hideous experience, and one I will regret putting up with until the day I die. I also think that if I do have some kind of deep seated psychological problem that prevents a decent orgasm, it can be traced back to Cock Features and his stupid elfin good looks.

He broke up with me by email, telling me he'd met someone else. He even had the gall to admit he'd been cheating on me with her the entire time.

Bastard.

I hate him for being such a scumbag - but if anything, I hate myself more for carrying on in a relationship with him.

Bugger it, I've decided Cock Features isn't bad enough. From now on I'm going to call him 'Fuck Face'.

6. Dan Dan, The Can Can Man.

I had sex with Dan Dan, The Can Can Man on holiday in Goa. To this day I have no idea why he was called Dan Dan, The Can Can Man, nor do I have a clue what his surname was. Hell, for all I know, his first name wasn't even Dan. What can I say? It was very hot out there and I drank far too much Cobra beer.

Dan Dan, The Can Can Man is the person who, up until now, has come closest to providing me with an orgasm during full intercourse, thanks to his marvellous technique and staying power. I'm fairly sure it would have happened, had the toilet in the bathroom next door not exploded. One second I'm rising on a wave of pleasure as Dan Dan thrusts into me, the next I'm screaming like a banshee as shards of porcelain came flying through the paper thin hostel bedroom wall.

I escaped unscathed, but Dan Dan got a rather nasty cut on his shoulder that would have probably become infected had I not packed a bottle of TCP in my luggage.

Much like the explanation for Dan Dan, The Can Can Man's nickname, I never found out why the toilet exploded. It was a holiday I will never, ever forget. Possibly for all the wrong reasons.

So, what's your diagnosis?

Have I just been unlucky in love? Or do I in fact have a malfunctioning sex drive?

Hard to tell, isn't it?

I've been repeatedly hit with the unlucky stick when it comes to the men in my life. The after effects of my early relationships may have had such a bad psychological impact on me (I'm thinking mainly of Fuck Face here) that my clitoris has shut up shop for the rest of my life, and will refuse to play ball no matter who I'm with.

But it surely can't be *that* cut and dry, can it?

Christina Hayley Enid Barclay can't be destined to never feel the thrill of her nerve endings on fire when, to put it bluntly, she's being impaled on a penis?

With my thirtieth birthday rapidly approaching, and working the kinds of shift patterns at the hospital that prevent much socialising, I was beginning to worry that my prayers may never be answered, and that I would indeed leave my twenties unsatisfied... and with cramp in my fingers.

Then, one night shortly before Christmas, a painfully inserted Ewok entered my life, bringing with it a new hope.

MATT

Matt Bunion is many things, but an experienced lover is not one of them.

On first dates, you usually spend time in stilted small talk, being cautious about revealing too much of yourself too early to the person in question, for fear of scaring them off with your inherent weirdness. Given that I had already removed a Star Wars action figure from young Mr Bunion's rectum, and had administered Christmas Eve first aid after he escaped from the clutches of a mentally unstable prostitute, I already knew he was *stupendously* weird, so he didn't bother with any pretence when we met in the local pub on a brisk second day in January.

'I'm a virgin,' he says with blunt and open honesty, over his pint of bitter shandy. 'All of my pre-Christmas insanity can be explained by this one hideous fact.'

'I see,' I reply carefully. 'And this is why you thought sticking an Ewok up your arse was a good idea? I hate to tell you this Matt, but that's not how you're supposed to lose your virginity.'

He gives me a withering look. 'It wasn't deliberate, I assure you.' He sighs. 'It was just one of many, *many* cock-ups I made in my desperate quest to pop my cherry.'

'Why so desperate?' I ask.

His face takes on the expression of a kicked puppy. 'I'm twenty seven, Christina!'

I pick up my Baileys and sip it thoughtfully. 'Yeah, I guess I can see how that might cause a man to do some rather stupid things.'

'You don't know the half of it.'

'No. I think it's probably better that we keep it that way if this is going to go anywhere.'

Oh God.

Did I really just say that?

Matt gives me a smile. It's a very nice smile, by all accounts.

If it weren't for the mass of black hair wobbling around on top of his head, the thick black glasses, and the slightly awkward way he carries himself, Matthew Bunion would be a draw to most women, I'm sure. I almost feel as if I've discovered a rich seam of gold that just needs some of the rough rock around it chipped away to reveal its shining glory. Matt appears completely unaware of the fact that he is actually a very handsome chap underneath all that nerd.

'I still can't believe we're sitting here having this conversation.' Matt says with a roll of his eyes. 'Usually when I meet a girl for the first time I just stammer a lot and ask her if she likes Star Trek. I've never admitted I'm a virgin before. I'd have been way too embarrassed.'

I shrug my shoulders. 'I've seen you naked from the waist down and rummaged around in your backside, Matt. I'd say we bypassed you needing to be embarrassed around me some time ago.'

Matt blushes red and suddenly looks very distressed. 'I wish you didn't know any of that stuff,' he says mournfully.

Damn.

I have a habit of doing this sometimes. Being an A&E nurse means feeling absolutely no awkwardness when it comes to discussing the human body. When you've spent most of your working life around bodies of all different sizes, shapes, colours and smells, you tend to forget that for most people, any discussion of human anatomy (especially when it's theirs) can be quite uncomfortable. I don't think my hairdresser will ever forgive me for talking about her vaginal discharge while she put the highlight foils in.

And now I've embarrassed Matt again by talking about his arsehole, a mere half an hour into our first proper date.

Damn.

I'd better do something to redress the balance here. This is currently a very one-sided conversation, with all the humiliating secrets coming from Matt's direction. I need to confide something to him, just to level things out a bit. A man's ego is fragile at the best of times, and if I don't want to scare Matt Bunion off completely, I'd better give him something back.

23

'I'll tell you a secret about myself if you like,' I say. 'To make things even.'

He laughs. 'What? You have some deep dark secret that can compete with me being a virgin and anal Ewok smuggler?'

I rock a hand back and forth. 'Maybe.'

'Go on,' he urges me. 'I have to know what it is now.'

I lean forward and look around conspiratorially. Matt does the same. 'I've never had an orgasm with a man in bed,' I whisper to him.

He looks non-plussed for a second. 'What's wrong with the bed?'

I roll my eyes. 'No... I don't mean I've never had an orgasm with a man *in a bed*. I mean I've never had an orgasm with a man *full stop*.'

Matt sits back again. 'Oh,' he says, the light dawning. 'Why's that then?'

'I don't know. Bad sex I guess?'

'Every time?'

'I suppose...'

He throws his hands up. 'Oh great! So what hope have I got then if I ever have sex with you?'

I arch one eyebrow in the archiest way possible. Matt catches its sudden archiness and his face blanches. 'Not that I'm assuming anything!' he wails.

I sip my drink and allow the eyebrow to drop a couple of millimetres. He does have a nice smile after all. 'We've all got things we're embarrassed about Matt, especially when it comes to the bedroom.'

'Fair enough. Thanks for confiding in me.' It looks like my gambit has worked, Matt seems instantly more at ease knowing that he's not the only one prepared to share his secrets.

I have to say, I find Matthew Bunion quite fascinating. I have never met anyone so awkward, skittish and naive in my life - but on the other hand he's clearly more intelligent, well-mannered and down to earth that the parade of unsuitables I've hooked up with in the past.

Maybe it's his total and complete lack of forced machismo. For some reason, most men seem compelled to play up their alpha male qualities as much as is humanly possible. I suppose there must be some Darwinian hunter-gatherer reasoning behind this, but it quite frankly makes my teeth ache, and I'm royally sick of it. Matt displays none of these characteristics, so I'm more than happy to see past the virginity and slight lack of social skills to the man underneath. He's got rough edges, but I'm sure I'll be able to smoo -

Oh God.

I've turned into one of those people, haven't I?

The type of person who wants to change someone right from the get-go; a control freak who isn't happy until their significant other wears the right clothes, attends the right social occasions, and doesn't speak out of turn at dinner parties.

In other words, I have become almost *every man I've ever dated.*

But what choice do I have? Matt is clearly in need of a little education, whether I want to provide it or not. If I don't give it a go with him, I'll be forced back onto the open market, which means I might bump into another Fuck Face. This will ensure an unsatisfactory sex life for years to come, until my untimely death on the end of a malfunctioning vibrator.

I decided a month was about the right amount of time to leave before curing Matt of his virginity problem.

Judging from his pre-Christmas exploits it was probably a good idea to break him in gently. If I'd jumped him too early he might have put me in the same category as the coffee table fiend, or the Cliff Richard obsessed hooker, and run a mile.

As it was, he managed to keep his nerves in check quite well on the following three dates we went on together. There was a slightly dodgy moment when I rested a hand on his knee in the cinema though. Thankfully the wild yelp of surprise he let out was muffled by Bruce Willis shooting someone with a machine gun, so we were spared any angry glances from our fellow movie going patrons.

It's an exquisitely strange sensation to be the one with the upper hand at the start of a relationship. I don't quite know what to do with it. I'm so used to being the twitchy one, that suddenly finding the tables turned in my favour is quite disconcerting. It's also rather empowering, so I'm not going to complain too much.

Matt wasn't complaining either, when I invited him to my house last Saturday night for a takeaway. This was the first time I had invited him to my place - where we would be alone, and close to a double bed. From the way his eyes bulged I could tell that the prospect of this excited and terrified him in equal measure. 'What would you prefer? Indian or Chinese?' I asked nonchalantly.

'Well...er, um, erm, er, um...' he replied helpfully. I folded my arms and sat back on the pub chair, knowing full well that this could take some time. Matt looked quite adorable as he sat there mulling over the difficult choice I'd presented him with. I think it was the way his hair bobbled about as he vibrated with indecision that made me smile more than anything. Either that, or the way he kept looking to the heavens for inspiration, with a slightly pained expression on his face.

Men really do lose their minds when the prospect of sex is on the cards. Doubly so when they haven't done it before, apparently.

Eventually I had to put him out of his misery. 'I think I'd like Chinese,' I said.

The hair bobbled up and down again, this time in rapid agreement. 'Yes, yes, yes, yes. Chinese sounds good. Very good. Chinese.'

It wasn't very good. It was decidedly average in fact, but I was starving after a busy day at work, so I shovelled in the chicken chow mein with gusto. Matt's mind was on other things, so the quality of the food didn't seem to bother him either. I'm fairly sure I could have plated up some fried cardboard and he wouldn't have noticed.

He *does* notice when I snake a speculative hand into his lap during Doctor Who though. It's testament to the power of sex that even a huge sci-fi geek like Matthew Bunion can be completely distracted from his favourite Time Lord by the attentions of a speculative hand. Okay, he does insist on Sky plussing the silly programme before concentrating on me completely, but we'll let him off because it's his first time.

Ten minutes of sofa kissing later, I'm ready to take things up a notch.

'Let's go upstairs,' I whisper in Matt's ear.

You know that thing dogs do when they're getting tickled on the tummy, and their back legs start to twitch? Men are much the same when you whisper into their ear.

I once got taught in physics that the speed of light is the fastest thing in the known universe, but in actual fact there is something faster: Matthew Bunion on his way up to my bedroom to have sex for the first time. I follow him at a much slower pace and close the door softly behind me when I reach the room. Matt sits on the bed and starts to look around nervously. 'This is a nice bedroom,' he says. 'Got lots of character.'

In fact, my bedroom is resolutely beige and contains just a king sized bed, a white wardrobe, a bedside cabinet, and a rubber pot plant on the window sill that I can't seem to kill, no matter how many times I forget to water it. This is a rental property, so there's no point in stamping my identity on it. I'm hardly ever here, thanks to how many shifts at work I'm having to do to pay for the place, so the minimalist look is fine by me.

I go over to the bed and sit next to my nervous date, taking his hand in mine, and kissing him gently. At first it's rather like kissing a shop dummy, but after a few moments Matt starts to relax, and things get a lot more enjoyable for the both of us. While Matt may be a virgin, it's plain he's had plenty of experience at foreplay, given that after five minutes he's going at it like a trained professional, and I'm flushing red from some very exciting neck nibbling.

'Wow. For a guy who says he's never had sex, you certainly know your way around a woman's body,' I gasp rather breathlessly as one Bunion hand runs its way up my thigh.

...and that will be the last time I refer to any part of Matt's anatomy using his surname. Nobody needs the visual image that my description of a 'Bunion penis' would create.

'I've had lots of practise at this bit,' Matt replies, neck nibbling again. 'It's the next section I've been having all the trouble with.'

'Then let's sort that little problem out right here and now, shall we?' I tell him and start to unzip my jeans.

Mere moments later we're both naked.

This is where things grind to a halt somewhat. Matt sits back from me on the edge of the bed and starts to squint around the room.

'What are you doing?' I ask.

'I'm checking for signs of catastrophic masonry failure.'

'Why exactly?'

'Well, something's got to go wrong, hasn't it? You're naked, I'm naked. There is absolutely nothing I can think of right now that would stop us actually having sex.' He looks up at the ceiling suspiciously. 'Therefore, some kind of unexpected disaster must be about to strike.' His eyes widen. 'When's the last time we had an earthquake?'

I lean forward. 'Nothing is going to happen, Matt.' I take hold of his penis in order to assuage his fears. 'Now, stop worrying and come here.'

I pull Matt down on top of me and wrap my hands around his tight little bottom. I have to admit there's a small part of my brain listening out for the sound of cracking brickwork, but I try to put it out of my head.

This task is made all the more easy when Matt slides into me with minimal effort. It's amazing how having an erect penis inside you can stop you thinking about anything, other than what it feels like to have an erect penis inside you.

I look up into Matt's eyes, which portray a look of stunned disbelief. 'Blimey,' he says.

My brow furrows. 'Blimey?' That's a little underwhelming, you know.'

'Sorry. I'm sure I'll sound more excited shortly, I'm just so amazed to be actually doing this that I think I've temporarily short circuited my brain.'

I give the side of Matt's head a playful slap. 'Then disengage your brain and start thinking with a lower part of your anatomy.'

Matt grins, kisses me, and starts to move his hips in a manner I find to be quite delicious.

Amazingly for a virgin, the sex is not over in three seconds flat. In fact, Matt starts to build up an extremely pleasurable rhythm that is as heart-stopping as it is unexpected. My breath starts to come in sharper and sharper gasps as his pace increases, and I suddenly find myself unable to formulate much coherent thought.

Could it be? Could it possibly be that I am about to have my first orgasm with a man? With a man who is having sex *for the first time*?

It certainly feels like it, as Matt gets faster, and starts to grunt in my ear. I let out a moan and throw my head back as another wave of pleasure hits me.

I can feel it *rising... rising...*

This is going to happen!

I'm going to cum!

I'm going to have an orgasm!

I'm going t -

Oh fuck it!

Matt lets out a loud startled cry as I feel him ejaculate.

No! No! No! I was so close!

But my silent protestations are for nought. Bunion has gone from a thrusting sexual dynamo, to a limp dishtowel in three nano-seconds flat. He flops down on top of me with an exhausted sigh. I try hard to contain a moan of disappointment.

I shouldn't feel this way of course. It's the poor lad's first time. What exactly was I expecting?

Nevertheless, I have come closer to a meaningful orgasm today than I have for years, so it's rather hard to ignore the deep sense of frustration as Matt slides off to one side and rolls onto his back, exhausted from his exertions.

To be fair to Mr Bunion, the subsequent crying is not entirely unexpected.

When you've spent most of your recent life obsessing about losing your virginity, it's understandable to get a bit emotional when it finally happens.

'There, there,' I say comfortingly, with an arm around his shoulder.

'Sorry,' he replies, wiping his nose. 'I'm just so relieved.'

'Not a problem. I completely understand. I felt much the same way after I passed my driving test.'

Matt looks at me speculatively. 'How was it for you?'

'Well, I thought I got a bit out of control on the parallel parking, but the instructor didn't seem to notice and passed me anyway.'

'I meant with the sex we've just had,' Matt replies, in an slightly exasperated tone.

Ah, the moment of sexual feedback. Always an inevitable part of a new relationship.

I affect what I like to call my expression of plastic happiness. It's the one I invariably end up trotting out whenever a man asks me that very question. 'I enjoyed it Matt,' I tell him, rather blandly.

'Did you... did you? You know... '

Now, at this point in the past I have lied easily. To stroke the man's ego, I have usually gone completely overboard and proclaimed it to be the best orgasm I've ever had, citing his enormous girth and expert technique for the reasons behind my extreme sexual gratification. Anyone thinking straight would have known I was lying, but a man who has just expelled his seed is often not the most astute of creatures, and will take whatever you say at face value, providing there's a cup of tea and a nap coming in the near future.

With Matt though, I feel like lying would be a betrayal somehow.

This is quite disconcerting. There may be more going on here than I first realised...

I shake my head and give him a lop-sided smile. 'Not this time, handsome. Sorry.'

His face immediately darkens. 'I'm the one who should be sorry.'

This is a sweet gesture, but entirely inappropriate. 'Don't worry about it, Matt. This was just the first time. I'm sure we'll have plenty more opportunities to sort my little issue out, now we've dealt with yours.'

The prospect of further sex lightens Matt's mood considerably - as does the cup of tea and nap he takes shortly afterwards.

I have to kick him out at eleven o'clock though, as I'm up early for work the next day.

'So, when can I see you again?' Matt asks on the doorstep as he is leaving.

'Next weekend?' I reply, knowing that I'll be wiped out from four upcoming twelve hour shifts anytime before then.

'Great!' he replies, and leans in for a kiss.

After we've locked lips again for a few moments, a look of such heartfelt gratitude crosses his face that it actually makes me feel more embarrassed than I was when confessing my lack of orgasmic experience to him in the pub. 'Thank you again,' he says. 'For, you know, sorting me out.'

'You make me sound like a chiropractor,' I reply with a smile.

'Oh God, sorry!'

I drag him back in for another kiss. 'Stop apologising, you big idiot. I enjoyed myself immensely, and am definitely looking forward to seeing you again.'

With this ringing endorsement in his ears, Matt Bunion ambles off down the front garden path and out into the street.

I'm left standing in the doorway with a rueful smile on my lips. I'm pleased to have got him over such a big hurdle in his life, but I'm still rather plagued by how close I came to jumping over my own this evening... ultimately with no success.

Maybe I'm bloody cursed.

It is with this troubling thought that I close the front door, go back into the bedroom, and start to warm my fingers up.

FIFTY SHADES OF BUNION

Over the next couple of weeks Matt and I saw each other as much as our schedules would allow. I have to say, each date was better than the last, and by the time Valentine's Day rolled around I was really enjoying myself with him.

However, as we all know, Valentine's Day is an *exquisitely* uncomfortable experience when you've been seeing someone for just a few short weeks. You can't brush it off completely, as that would send out entirely the wrong signals to the other person. But equally, you can't make too much of a big deal of the occasion, otherwise you will come across as a crazed bunny boiler. It's a tricky one.

As Matt and I have developed a relationship based on a refreshing amount of up front honesty, the issue was dealt with neatly in the following conversation:

'I hate Valentine's Day,' says he.

'Me too,' says I.

'Shall we just ignore it, stay out of contact for twenty four hours to avoid awkwardness, and see each other the next day, when all the restaurants have stopped charging double?'

'That's an *excellent* idea, Matt!'

And so it was that Christina Barclay spent Valentine's Day sat happily on the sofa watching Gerard Butler movies, dressed in her fluffiest of fluffy blue dressing gowns, and drinking far too much red wine.

It is, without doubt, the best Valentine's Day I've ever had, including the nice one I spent in Tenerife with Simon Addison that started well, but went downhill once he suggested going to the nice local karaoke bar. No-one, and I mean *no-one*, needs to hear me destroy *Love Lifts Us Up Where We Belong* on the most romantic day of the year. I couldn't have ruined the atmosphere in the bar more if I'd stuck my fingers down my throat at the end of the song and vomited into a pint glass.

Matt did text me right in the middle of my eighth viewing of *300* to say he was thinking of me, and was slightly drunk in the pub with his friends. He told me he was looking forward to seeing me the next night, when he wouldn't be surrounded by idiots who kept on insisting that The Matrix Reloaded wasn't that bad a movie after all. I replied, wishing him well in his protracted argument, and ended the text by telling him I was looking forward to seeing him as well. It takes a lot to distract me from a Gerard Butler film (especially one where is he dressed in very little, other than a codpiece and helmet) so it's a testament to my interest levels in Mr Bunion that I didn't wait to respond to his text until after the movie had finished.

I spend my first evening in Matt's flat the following night.

Until now this has been a no-go area, given that a man in his late twenties who lives alone, is slightly less hygienic than a brain damaged pig. Matt had forked out for a cleaner to come over during the day though, so by the time I get there at 7.30pm, the whole flat smells of lavender and peach blossom. The carpets have also been scrubbed to within an inch of their lives, and it requires sunglasses to step into the gleaming kitchen. Okay, the walls are still covered in sci-fi movie posters, the doorbell still plays the Imperial March from Star Wars, and there is (for some reason) a statue of a giant plastic duck wearing combat trousers in his bedroom, but on the whole Matt has gone to a great deal of effort tonight, which I'm extremely grateful for.

We'll still be ordering an Indian though. While the cooker is cleaner than it has been in decades, it's still rustier than the railings on the Titanic, and I don't really fancy baking anything in it, for fear of inadvertently tripling my daily iron intake.

'The place looks lovely Matt,' I tell him, more or less honestly as he gives me a brief guided tour.

'Pfft,' he replies, 'It looks habitable, which is about the best you can expect without extensive redecoration. Yelena is great, but there's only so much one Slovakian woman can do in three hours on a Saturday afternoon. I tipped her handsomely just for getting rid of that stain in the bathroom I've been too terrified to go near.'

'Well, you've made an effort, which wins you lots of brownie points, young man.'

Young man?

I cringe inwardly. I've just spoken to my new boyfriend the way a boarding school head mistress would talk to one of the more unruly boys, who has finally handed in a decent piece of English homework. It must be the age gap. Or the experience gap. Or both.

Matt may actually be only three years younger than me, but the giant plastic duck and Star Wars doorbell regress him even further in my mind.

He doesn't seem to notice my impression of a schoolmarm though, thank God. I know that some men go in for that kind of thing, but this is not the type of woman who would go in for *them*.

What I do like to go in for though is a kiss, which is what I do while we're waiting for the takeaway to arrive. Several kisses in fact. And some light fondling. I'm sure we'll be getting on to the more energetic stuff later, but there's nothing wrong with whetting your appetite early, in my book.

All is going swimmingly until Matt breaks away with a thoughtful look on his face.

'What's up?' I ask with concern. I don't like it when people look at me thoughtfully. No good can come of it.

Matt shuffles uncomfortably and has trouble meeting my gaze.

Really?

I'm getting dumped *already*?

How will my ego get over this one, eh? He's an awkward sci-fi nerd in his late twenties who's only just been relieved of his virginity. Where exactly do I go from here if I can't keep hold of this guy?

'What's the matter, Matt?' I repeat, with a sinking heart.

'I've been thinking about your problem,' he says in a quiet voice.

'What problem?'

'You know... with not having an orgasm when you're with me.'

I sigh. Well, at least I'm not getting dumped. It does appear that some ego massaging is in order though, which I could really do without, to be honest. 'It's not just with *you*, Matt. I told you, it's something I've always had issues with, no matter who it is I've slept - '

'Yeah! I know!' He holds out his hands to stop me. 'Don't worry, I'm not being insecure about myself or anything. This isn't about my ego.'

The boy may be inexperienced, and have hair that only a hedge trimmer could love, but he's also very astute when the mood takes him.

'Then why do you bring it up, when you could be nibbling my neck?'

This brings out a shy smile, which is a much nicer alternative to the thoughtful look. 'I've... I've been doing a bit of research.'

'Into what?'

'Er... women's orgasms.'

My eyes narrow. 'If this is your way of admitting that you like looking at porn Matt, I'm not your mother, you can look at what you like as long as there are no farm animals involved.'

He shakes his head. 'No, no, no. I don't mean that.' He grabs his iPad. 'I mean I've been looking at some sites that give advice to women who have trouble reaching a climax and - '

'Whoa boy!' My turn to hold out the hands. 'I'll stop you right there. I'm a nurse, remember? I've done all the research myself. There's nothing wrong with my bits and pieces. It's all up here in my noggin.' I poke myself in the temple, by way of explanation.

Matt nods quickly. 'I figured as much. You'd be on top of anything medical, I know. But if you are having issues with your, um, noggin, then it might be a good idea to shake things up a bit.' He points at the open Safari page on his iPad. 'Some of these sites suggest that being stuck in a sexual rut could be the issue, so to speak. They suggest trying, um, *new things* to see if that helps.'

'New things?'

'Yeah, you know... sex wise.'

I'm not sure this is the *wisest* conversation to be having before *sex*, but I'm willing to give him a chance, as he's obviously been thinking about this a lot - which is very sweet when you get right down to it. 'What sort of *new things*?' I ask.

Matt flushes red. 'Kinky stuff.'

'Kinky stuff?'

'Yeah. Toys, a bit of bondage, role-playing. That kind of malarkey.'

'That kind of *malarkey*?'

'Yeah. I just thought you might like to try some new things out. I know what it's like to have a deadline on something important, and I'd like to help you meet yours, even though I missed mine by a few weeks. If that means doing some, er, more kinky stuff, then I'm up for it.'

'I don't have a deadline, Matt, What are you talking about?'

'Well, you said you'd never had an orgasm with a man, and that you'd like it to happen before your birthday at Easter, so...' Matt trails off, uncertain how to finish such a ridiculous sentence.

I roll my eyes. Why do men have to turn everything into some kind of epic challenge? 'So, you figured that because you set yourself the goal of losing your virginity before Christmas Day, I might want to do similar with my orgasmic issues, yes?'

'Pretty much.'

I slap him on the shoulder. 'Oh for crying out loud, Matt!'

'I'm sorry! I just thought you might like the idea.' He shrugs his shoulders. 'After all, it might turn out to be fun, and what have you got to lose?'

I'm spared the task of thinking about what I've got to lose by the sound of the doorbell heralding the arrival of our curry... and a blessed end to this idiotic conversation.

43

However, as I make my way through the chicken jalfrezi and keema naan, I start thinking about Matt's last words on the subject.

What, indeed, do I have to lose?

I can't pretend that a few 'alternative' sexual methods don't sound interesting, and even if it doesn't cure me of my orgasmic drought, it sounds like it'd be a lot of fun anyway. I've never been one for anything other than straightforward sex before, and it never occurred to me that by experimenting a little I might find a way around the roadblock.

Also, it's not as if Matt is any kind of expert when it comes to this type of thing either. He'll be just as much a novice as me.

'You're thinking about it, aren't you?' Matt says mischievously over a forkful of pilau rice.

'Possibly,' I respond, popping a lump of what I hope is chicken into my mouth.

He puts down the fork and cocks his head to one side. 'Well... if you fancy having a go at something tonight, I may well have bought a few things.'

I'm flabbergasted. 'You've bought a load of sex stuff? How did you work up the courage to do that?'

'You'd be amazed what you can get on Amazon these days. The one day delivery service is fantastic.'

'Oh, good grief.'

'What do you say we finish our curry and then maybe go into the bedroom? I can show you what I bought and see if you're, you know, interested in any of it?'

I give him a suspicious look. 'Are you sure all of this isn't just one big ploy to get me to do all the dirty stuff you've fantasised about since you were eighteen?'

Matt smiles broadly. 'Of course it is! But only as a side issue. I really would like to help you, the way you helped me Christina.' He takes my hand and his voice drops to a mumble. 'I really do like you a lot.'

And you know what? I think he really does.

I'm not sure I'm entirely behind this rather leftfield idea, but I am willing to give it a try. He's just so bloody earnest - with his big silly hair, thick spectacles and near constant expression of good natured befuddlement.

I put my fork down and take a swig of wine, before standing up from the table. 'Come on then, lover boy, let's see what you've got in store for me.'

'Now?'

'Yes, *now*. I'm pretty much done with eating rubbery chicken for one evening, and my curiosity is piqued.'

'Oh right. Yes. Okay,' Matt says, flushing red again.

Sigh.

If he's going to get this embarrassed before we've even made it to the bedroom, I fear this little experiment of his won't be over until I reach my fortieth.

'What on God's Green Earth do you expect me to do with that?!' I exclaim in no uncertain terms, as Matt produces a foot long torpedo shaped piece of aquamarine ghastliness from the Amazon packaging box. It is *mesmerisingly* large. So much so that even Big Rob Pottinger would feel emasculated by it. Half way down its considerable length is a bulgy see-through section containing a load of ball bearings. The handle is chromed and replete with several shiny buttons and knobs.

It looks less like a sex toy, and more like something Darth Vader would clean his fish tank with.

'You don't like the look of it then?' Matt says, a bit crestfallen.

'As a weapon I can fight off burglars with, yes. As something to introduce into my sex life, and my vagina, forget about it.'

'All the customer reviews said it was very good,' Matt says in defence of his choice.

'Do they? I'm amazed any of them had the strength to power up the computer.'

'So, this one's out then?'

'I'd say so, yes.'

Matt slips the chrome and blue monstrosity back into the box and produces something much smaller. 'How about this little fella, then?' he says and holds up what looks like a miniature pink rabbit sat on a hula hoop. The small rubber rabbit has a slightly perplexed expression on his face, as if he is surprised to find himself atop a hula hoop - and not in his more customary domain of a hole in the ground.

'It looks less likely to cause me internal injuries, so that's a start,' I reply cautiously.

'It's called a Buzzing Bunny. I slip it over... myself, and then turn it on with this button here.' Matt provides me with a demonstration by sliding the toy over three of his fingers and clicking the button just under the rabbit. The whole thing starts to buzz and wobble back and forth. If the rabbit was perplexed before, it now looks mildly terrified as well, thanks to the vibration effect. 'The idea is that the rabbit's ears touch you on the clitoris while we make love.'

Time for me to do some eye rolling again. 'Yes Matt, it's a bloody cock ring. I know how they work. Just because I've not used these things before, doesn't mean I'm not fully aware of what they are. Nurse, remember?'

'Good point. Sorry.'

I place one finger on the end of the rabbit's ears. The sensation is not unpleasant. 'I'm certainly more willing to give this one a go though.'

'Great!'

'What else have you got in your magic box of filth, then?'

Matt gives me a disparaging look, but removes the Buzzing Bunny before delving into the box for a final time. He produces what looks like the kind of thing they use on people in Guantanamo Bay. 'That's a bondage kit, isn't it?' I say to him.

'Yep! An under the bed bondage kit, actually.' He holds up four velvet covered cuffs attached to several long black nylon straps. 'I thought I could tie you up!'

'Did you?'

'Yeah. This is supposed to be *really* sexy too. You just lie on the bed, tied up so you can't move, and I do lots of stuff to you. It should be fantastic!'

I take the bondage kit from Matt's sweaty grasp. 'It sounds like a nice idea, but there is *one* rather fundamental change I think I'd like to make to it... '

The last Velcro cuff goes around Matt's left ankle, and I sit back to admire my handiwork. 'Comfortable?' I say to a very naked and tied down Mr Bunion.

Matt's face crumples. 'It's not entirely what I had in mind when I clicked on the one-day delivery button, if I'm honest.'

'I bet it isn't.'

He looks up at the tight straps that hold his arms out straight. They disappear under the bed where they fasten together. 'To be frank, the whole thing is a bit disconcerting.'

Not from where I'm sitting. From where I'm sitting, I have a helpless, naked, and attractive man all to myself. A small and unexpected shiver of excitement runs through me. 'Let me see if I can make it less disconcerting for you,' I tell him in a husky voice, and grab the one extremity on his body not tied down with a Velcro cuff.

Within a few seconds little Bunion is standing proud and doing a passable imitation of a sun dial. I continue to maintain his happy state by increasing the speed of my hand, which causes him to test the strength of those Velcro cuffs most satisfactorily.

Oh my.

Who'd have thought it? That Christina Barclay, a girl who has never thought of herself as a dominatrix-type, is enjoying having a man under her complete control? One tied down to a bed and helpless!

Usually, when I'm dealing with someone lying on a bed, it's to change a dressing, or possibly to remove a bedpan - two things that couldn't be further away from being sexy if they tried. It comes as something as a surprise to be turned on quite as much as I am.

'Just call me Christina Grey,' I say with a giggle.

'Who?'

'You know, like the guy from that book?'

Matt stares at me blankly. 'What guy? What book?'

'Never mind.' I guess I shouldn't be entirely unsurprised that a sci-fi geek like Matt has no idea what I'm on about.

To put things back on track, I kiss the end of his penis and smile wickedly. 'I think I need to get naked too,' I tell him, and divest myself of all my clothing.

'Do you... do you want to try the buzzing bunny?' he asks, catching his breath.

I hesitate for a moment. Right now, I'm enjoying this bit of light experimentation, but I don't know whether the introduction of a battery operated piece of apparatus is necessarily the best move.

Then again, I never thought bondage was my thing, but apparently it is, so why not give the perplexed looking bunny a go, and see what all the fuss is about?

I pick up the toy from Matt's bedside cabinet and slip it over him. When I flick the switch on he lets out a whimper. 'Blimey, that's a interesting sensation,' he says with eyes wide.

It certainly *looks* interesting. It looks rather bizarre too. The bunny wobbles and vibrates at the base of his penis, looking for all the world like it's about to climb up it like a tree trunk. Nestled as the rabbit is in his pubic hair, it reminds me of the cover of *Watership Down*. This automatically makes my stupid brain start singing *Bright Eyes*, which, let me tell you, is not the kind of song you want in your head when you're contemplating the mounting of an erect penis. The phrase 'burning like fire' should not be one on the tip of your tongue whenever genitals are involved. It throws up a whole series of unpleasant images, along with the memory of a lengthy and embarrassing trip to the gynaecologist.

To try and get the heart-breaking song and movie out of my head, I throw my leg over Matt's body and rest my crotch up against his vibrating manhood.

'Wow,' I exclaim breathlessly.

'Does it feel good?'

'Um... yeah. It feels *very* good.'

And I haven't even climbed on properly yet. The next few minutes of my life promise to be *highly* memorable.

Taking things very slowly, I lower myself down onto Matt. I stop just as the bunny's ears are about to touch parts of my anatomy that have previously only been caressed by fingers and the occasional poorly trained tongue. This is something of a watershed moment. One that I should probably try to enjoy and not get too carried aw -

JESUS CHRIST! JESUS CHRIST ON A BIKE, WITH A CROSS-EYED BUNNY UNDER EACH ARM!

It's like someone has simultaneously poked me with an electrified cattle prod, *and* just told me I can have a two month holiday in the Caribbean for free.

'Huuuuurrrnnnnnnnn,' I say to no-one in particular.

'Good?' Matt asks.

Good? GOOD?

The last time I ate a Marks and Spencer's Eton Mess it was *good*. This is a feeling that words haven't as yet been invented to describe.

When they are, they will be long, have many syllables, and will have to be shouted through a loudhailer from the top of Mount Everest.

Oh, small buzzing pink bunny, where the hell have you been all my life?

I try to move up and down on Matt, which makes the sensation even stronger. I have to stop, as I just don't have the motor skills to accomplish even such a simple task right now. My thighs have turned to jelly. Matt seems to sense my pleasurable predicament, and starts to do some of the heavy lifting for me, moving his hips slowly up and down while I remain more or less immobile on top.

It is the most exquisitely wonderful feeling I have ever had.

It is also a stone cold guarantee that I will very shortly be achieving my first orgasm with a man inside me. To be honest, a department store dummy would probably reach a climax with a little pink buzzing friend like this placed against it. In the next few moments the floodgates will open... never to be closed again!

I moan long and loud, as Matt continues to move beneath me.

Ahhhhhhhh...

Ohhhhhhhhhhhhhhhh...

Ahhhhhhhhhhhhhhhhhhhhhhhhhhh...

Ohhhhhhhhhhhhhhhhhhhhhhhhhhhhhhhhhhhhhhhh-

hang on a bloody moment...

Something doesn't feel right.

The pleasure centres of my brain are starting to register a rather uncomfortable feeling that has started in my left leg, on the inside of my thigh. It's a weird fluttering sensation that I don't like in the slightest.

It's a feeling I've not had for a very long time. As the memory of it blasts through the haze of sexual excitement, I feel my blood run cold.

Let's go back fourteen years, shall we? To Christina Barclay's first ride on a motorcycle...

Said motorcycle was owned by Charlie, a ne'er-do-well from the council estate down the road, who had taken a fancy to me in art class at school. Charlie liked to ride around on a small but energetic motorbike that he'd won in a bet. The bet had been to see who could eat the most cigarettes in one minute, so he'd really earned that little 90cc motor.

He took me out for a ride deep into the nearby forest for some light teenage fumbling, which my adolescent body and mind had enjoyed immensely. Less enjoyable were the terrible vibrations that 90cc engine sent powering through my legs on the half an hour ride back to my house. By the time we turned into my street I could feel a horrible fluttering sensation making its way up my inner thigh. I managed to say a hurried goodbye to Charlie at my front gate, before hobbling up the garden path and slamming the door behind me.

In my room I then suffered the most painful cramp imaginable. My father nearly broke the door in half trying to get to me to see what all the screaming was about, and then almost went looking for Charlie to break *him* in half, until I explained about the motorcycle's vibrations giving me the cramp, rather than any part of poor Charlie's anatomy.

I was banned from ever seeing Charlie again, which was upsetting. I was also banned from riding a motorcycle, which was not.

And here I am, almost a decade and a half later, with the same warning flutter running up my leg.

I know what's coming.

It isn't going to be *me*.

'Matt,' I bark in a strangled voice.

'What?'

'I have to... I have to get off!'

Matt isn't far away from his intended destination either, so is understandably distraught at my reluctance to continue. 'Just a few more moments! I'm nearly there!'

'No Matt! I have to stop now before it's too late and I start cra - '

But, of course, it *is* too late.

The cramp seizes my entire left leg. It feels like somebody with a real grudge against me has decided to pour petrol over my leg and set it on fire.

'Aaaargggh!' I wail and clutch at my burning thigh. With Herculean effort considering the agony I'm in, I pull myself off Matt and fall to one side. In doing so I neatly smack one of Matt's testicles with my heel.

'Aaaargggh!' he echoes, the cords standing out on his neck as he thrashes in pain against the constraints.

I would like to administer some kind of first aid to him, but I am now face down on the bed, both hands wrapped around my leg, willing the cramp to subside.

It does not co-operate, so I am forced to roll over and sit up. My only recourse of action is to get off the bed, and try to walk around to get the blood flowing again.

Matt is still thrashing around in pain, trying in vain to release himself from the straps so he can clasp his hands around his poor abused testicle. This distressing vision is made more comical than it should be, by the little pink buzzing rabbit still vibrating back and forth at the base of his penis. 'Ow! Ow!' he screeches. 'Why did you do that? I know we were... we were trying a bit of bondage, but I'm not into pain!'

'I didn't do it deliberately, you pillock!' I spit as I rise unsteadily to my feet. 'I've got a bloody cramp!'

'What? In your vagina?'

Even in my agony, I can't let that stupendously idiotic pronouncement go unpunished. 'Yes, Matt. I have a cramping fanny,' I say with pained sarcasm dripping from every syllable. 'It's quite common, but I'll just go pour some water on it and give it a squeeze. I'm sure it will be fine.'

'Really?'

'No! Not fucking *really*, you giant bell end! It's in my bloody thigh. The bunny set it off.' I start to hobble towards the end of the bed, still kneading at my thigh as I go.

'What did it do?' Matt asks, as if it had come alive and started molesting me.

'The vibration, I mean!'

'Is there anything I can do?'

I don't want to glare at him. His offer of help is perfectly reasonable, but wracking pain never puts me in a particularly grateful mood, so poor old Matt gets the full force of my ocular displeasure. 'There's nothing you can do. I just... just need to walk around a bit to get the blood flowing again.'

After freeing Matt's hands from the bondage straps, I spend the next ten minutes hobbling like a geriatric pirate around a bedroom containing more Star Wars memorabilia than is strictly necessary for any one human being.

Thankfully, after much puffing, panting, swearing and moaning, the cramp loosens off enough for me to sit back down with a half sigh of relief.

'Um. I don't think my ball is quite right,' Matt says, uncupping himself so I can get a look.

Even if I wasn't a trained nurse, I could quite easily tell that Matt is right, as his testicle now resembles a blood orange. In size and texture anyway. 'God! Why didn't you say something?!'

The look of puppy dog like sorrow is as heartbreaking as it is guilt inducing. 'I didn't want to interrupt you while you were cramping.'

Right then, so instead of achieving a nerve-jangling orgasm this evening thanks to a pink buzzing bunny, I instead get to achieve soul-blackening guilt thanks to a swollen testicle. 'We'd better get you to A&E,' I say with a sinking feeling. '...again,' I add, completely unnecessarily.

Luckily, Matt hasn't suffered any permanent damage. The testicle is a fragile little thing though, and doesn't react well to being walloped with a heel. According to Travis the junior doctor - who I know for a fact is banging the 43 year old head of the x-ray department - it'll be a few days before the swelling goes down, but other than that Matt will make a complete recovery.

'That could have gone better really,' my wounded boyfriend says from the passenger seat of the car as we pull back up at his flat three hours later.

'Indeed,' I say, still wincing as I climb out of the car. The cramp may have gone, but the residual ache won't be going anywhere for a couple of days yet.

'Still, you've got to look on the bright side,' he continues, gingerly getting out of the car himself.

'How's that exactly?'

'At least I haven't had anything rammed up my arse this time. I should be able to sit down okay, which makes a nice change.'

I take Matt's arm and we shamble together up the garden path to the front door. We look for all the world like two soldiers returning home from years of combat, rather than two people who just tried something kinky in bed.

'I need some sleep,' Matt yawns contagiously.

We make our slow and pained way back to his bedroom, to discover that while we have been gone, the buzzing bunny has leaked battery fluid all over the duvet.

This rather says it all, when you get right down to it.

I thank my lucky stars that we didn't try anything *really* adventurous this evening. If we'd have broken out a sex swing or a set of anal beads, there's every possibility we'd now both be crippled for life... or stone cold dead.

PUBLIC INDECENCY FOR BEGINNERS

What a glorious thing annual leave truly is. Especially when it coincides with the first period of good weather we've had since last September.

I have a whole five days off, and Spring has most definitely sprung, with a healthy dose of late March sun bathing the country in a rosy glow that makes you glad to be alive.

I had planned on doing precisely bugger all the entire time.

This was the first decent period of leave I'd had in six months, and I intended to take advantage of it to the fullest - by being so astronomically lazy that God himself would look down on me in shame, and wish he'd never bothered with any life form more complicated than a radish.

Matthew Bunion has other plans in store for me though.

You'd think that a cramping thigh and a swollen bollock might put paid to a relationship only in its early stages - and with any other couple, you'd be absolutely right. As it is, once our respective injuries had healed up, we got right back on the horse... so to speak. I have increased my life insurance premium though, just to be extra safe.

'What are you doing over the weekend?' Matt asks excitedly, the second he's in the house. It's Thursday night, the end of my first day off, and I'm already more relaxed than I have been in weeks. The glass of red wine I have clutched in my hand has everything to do with this.

'Absolutely nothing,' I reply with a smile. 'A big massive pile of fuck all.'

'Ah, right. Great!' Matt claps his hands together and favours me with an expectant grin. 'Have you ever been to Scotland?'

'What?'

'Scotland? Have you ever been there?'

'No. Why?' I ask warily, having a feeling I know what's coming.

Yep, out come the tickets from his pocket.

Crap.

It's an absolutely lovely gesture, but I'd much rather just swan around the house for four days in my dressing gown.

'I've booked us a weekend away!' Matt says excitedly.

'Really!?' I exclaim, trying to sound happier than I actually am.

'Yeah! Surprise!'

I put down the wine, wrap my arms around Matt and give him a big kiss. 'Thank you. It's a lovely present,' I tell him, maintaining my show of enthusiasm.

My faked excitement is replaced by the genuine sort when he shows me the place we'll be staying at on his phone. It's a five star spa called The McInnish Resort, which nestles in the Highlands next to Loch Lomond. If the pictures on the website are anything to go by, my relaxing weekend will now be accentuated by an infinity pool, a cocktail bar the size of my entire house, and the kind of beautiful scenery that will literally take your breath away if you climb high enough up it.

'How much did this cost?' I ask in disbelief, as I take in the majesty of the Nordic sauna, and a la carte restaurant.

'A fair bit!' Matt says, with a slightly wild look in his eyes.

My new boyfriend works in a relatively small I.T company, so my next question is to be expected. 'How can you afford it?'

Matt rocks his head from side to side. 'Well, I kinda sold a couple of my posters on Ebay. The Japanese Star Wars one, and the original Toho Godzilla one from the fifties.'

I know as much about sci-fi memorabilia as I do yak farming, but even I'm aware of how much rare posters like that can sell for. I feel tears pricking my eyes. I'm well aware what those posters meant to him, so the fact he'd sold them to take me away for the weekend is amazing.

'Thank you, Matt. Thank you so much.' No need to feign any emotions this time around.

'You're welcome! I'm looking forward to it myself. There are lots of walks you can do around the area. Plenty to see and do.'

While the prospect of tramping around the Scottish countryside doesn't fill me with as much joy as the Nordic sauna and a la carte restaurant, I'm still very excited about my first visit to the Highlands. If Matt wants to take me on a walk through scented pine forests and across babbling brooks then I'm not going to complain, as long as there is someone back at the hotel ready and willing to massage my feet upon my return.

'We fly tomorrow morning, so you'd best get packing,' Matt tells me.

'Okay. I'll get started in about twenty minutes.'

'What are you going to do before then?'

By way of explanation, I remove my t-shirt and start to nibble on one of his earlobes.

Sadly, the sex still doesn't end with me having an orgasm, but I am about to stay in a five star spa resort, where all my smallest whims will be catered for, so all in all I'm more than happy to put this evening down in the win column.

The flight from Gatwick to Glasgow goes very smoothly the next morning, and before you know it we're driving the hire car towards Loch Lomond through tree-lined mountains, warmed by spectacular Spring sunshine.

When the Loch itself comes into view I let out a gasp of sheer delight. The sun makes the millpond smooth water of the vast Loch twinkle like it's alive with fireflies. I have never seen anything quite so beautiful in my life, and I therefore spend the next five minutes taking two hundred photos of exactly the same thing, until my thumb starts to ache and my phone's battery dies.

Which is a real shame, as it means I can't take another two hundred photos of the glorious McInnish spa resort as we drive up the wide sweeping gravel road that leads to it. It is every inch the dramatic Scottish manor house, built from grey stone and replete with more buttresses and crenulations than you can shake a stick at. This bugger has *turrets*, people. Proper pointy turrets.

It also has someone to take your bags when you arrive, which I am very grateful for, as I have packed enough clothes to last me six months. It may well be unseasonably warm right now in the Scottish Highlands, but I've seen *Take The High Road*, and I know the weather can change in a heartbeat. I don't fancy freezing to death over my last piece of shortbread.

'Wow,' Matt exclaims as we enter the foyer of the hotel. It's an expensive combination of old school Scottishness, and ultra modern styling. Who'd have thought dark stained oak panels would go so well with uplighters and polished marble?

I'm the one wowing when we're shown to our room.

There is one brief shining moment in life when you have just finished an extensive Spring clean of your house, and you stand back to admire just how clean, neat and tidy the front room is for the first time in months. Your freshly cleaned lounge would still look like a shithole compared to how wonderful this hotel room is.

It feels like they've just taken the wrappers off everything. I want to build myself a nest of fluffy towels on the enormous king sized bed and order room service until Judgement Day arrives.

'The shower has one of those rain heads,' Matt points out happily. 'You know a place is swanky when it has a rain shower.'

If anything, the rest of the hotel and spa makes our room look like a doss house. They might as well have wallpapered the place in twenty pound notes, judging by the cost of all the interior design. A small but perky Scottish girl called Linda gives us the guided tour of the place, taking in the restaurant, swimming pool, spa treatment rooms and cocktail bar. The Nordic sauna looks even better in real life, as does the view from the enormous veranda that overlooks Loch Lomond.

'I have to move here,' I tell Matt on the way back to our room. 'Did you bring that bondage kit along? I want to shackle myself to the radiator so they can never throw me out.'

The next two days pass in a blissful haze of utter gloriousness that I find hard to believe. Highlights include the aforementioned sauna - which does wonders for my pores; the Thai back massage - which does equal wonders for the bad back I've had since I had to catch a drunk eighteen stone man at work two months ago; and a salted caramel & chocolate pudding that I would cheerfully eat until I dropped into a coma - when I would continue to have the pudding intravenously injected into my body.

It's amazing how much time you can waste sat on a veranda in the Spring sunshine while someone brings you mojitos ...and more salted caramel & chocolate pudding.

By the time Sunday morning rolls around I am so relaxed there's every danger my brain is about to trickle out of my ears.

Matt however, is feeling rather restless it seems. My job has me on my feet all day, whereas his keeps him bound to a desk most of the time. No surprise then, that after two days of doing bugger all, he's feeling a tad fidgety.

'Do you fancy going for a walk?' I ask him, noticing how his leg is twitching up and down on the recliner next to me.

His eyes light up. 'Yeah! That'd be great. There's a good one that winds up into the mountain behind us. We can start it right here.'

I look down at my pampered and soft feet. 'How long is it?'

'Oh, a couple of miles... I think.'

I don't necessarily like the sound of that '*I think*' but I'm willing to give it a go. This is as much Matt's trip as it is mine, and he did pay for it, so it's only fair to do something he fancies. Besides, I have to walk off all that bloody salted caramel & chocolate pudding at some point, don't I?

'Okay, let me finish my coffee, and we'll get dressed and go.'

'Great!' Matt is up like a shot and heading back towards the hotel before I've had chance to say anything else. I really do hope this walk calms him down a bit. I fully intend to spend my last evening here in the sauna until my bodily fluids drop to dangerously low levels, so I want him nice and content beforehand.

I am extremely proud of my walking ensemble. I definitely think I look like someone ready and prepared to ramble their way around the peaks and valleys of the Scottish Highlands. Like every soft southern tourist who thinks this though, I am completely deluded. Fat Face combat trousers, a Republic hoodie and Caterpillar boots are entirely unsuitable for the kinds of weather and terrain Scotland can throw at you. But I look cute as a button, dammit.

Thankfully, the mini-heat wave has extended right through the weekend, so I should just about get away with it.

Matt might well be even worse off, given that he's wearing ordinary blue jeans, a pair of crunchy Doc Martins and an Avengers t-shirt. He looks happy as we set off though, so I don't choose to point out that if a change comes in the weather, there's nothing Robert Downey Jnr and The Incredible Hulk can do to stop him freezing to death.

The walk begins on a gentle uphill slope from the hotel's car park. It wends its way between the trees and beside the Loch for a good five hundred metres, before turning left and continuing upwards on a pleasantly shallow incline. As we walk, butterflies flutter around our heads, the birds sing in the trees, and the midgies (thanks to the repellent we've just slathered ourselves in) stay out of arm's reach, knowing what's good for them.

I am in rambling heaven. The hustle, stress and exhaustion of the A&E department feels a world away.

I smile broadly at an elderly couple who pass us going the other way. They are both dressed in neat Highland tweed and have a portly, huffing Beagle dog with them, who comes to investigate my legs. I give him a friendly pat and a tickle behind the ears. My Disney-like levels of *Zip-dee-doo-dah* contentment obviously translate down to the chubby dog, as he gives me a gentle, happy lick on the fingers before ambling back to his owners - who issue Matt and I with a friendly hello, before continuing on their way.

'Enjoying yourself?' Matt asks a few minutes later, noticing my broad, indulged smile. We've just come round a corner of the path and can now look right across the Loch, which still dazzles in the sunlight.

'Oh God yes. Thanks for bringing me here,' I say and give him a kiss. He snakes an arm around my waist and presses into me. The kiss becomes a lingering one that lasts a full minute.

This makes me more horny than a rhino playing the trumpet.

When we get back to the hotel room, Matt will be receiving my attentions to a leg trembling degree.

Sadly, this new found rampant horniness rather puts me off my stride. Where I was previously enjoying the pleasant scenery around me, now all I can think about is sex. The glorious Highland countryside is now completely lost on me. I might as well be walking through the centre of Middlesbrough. I want to be back at the McInnish spa, removing that silly Avengers t-shirt from Matt, and showing him what's under my Republic hoodie.

I'm so lost in my own sexual reverie that I barely notice how the track has started to steepen as we ascend further up the side of the mountain. We're now walking through a heavy pine forest that is as silent as the grave.

'Wow. It feels really isolated in here,' Matt points out.

'Yeah, it does,' I reply, looking up and down the path and not seeing another soul. 'Nobody else about.'

Matt nods. 'We're completely alone. What a strange feeling.' He looks up. 'Shame the trees are blocking out the sunlight.'

'Not over there, they're not,' I say, and point to an open glade about fifty feet off the path to our left. It's ringed by trees, so a lot of it is obscured, but I can see that the open grass area is sun dappled, and extremely picturesque. 'Looks beautiful, doesn't it?'

Now, I'm sure you are one step ahead of me here - especially those of you who have entertained yourselves with a little outdoor sex in the past.

The setting is perfect, I am hornier than a sixteen year old girl, and I have a man with me who is ready, willing and able.

These three very important facts are all crowding themselves at the front of my brain, and any second now I'm going to connect the dots.

Wait for it...

Wait for it...

'Matt!' I exclaim, eyes widening.

'What?'

'Er... why don't we go stand in the sunny bit?'

'What for? It looks a bit undergrowthy over there. I don't want to get muddy.'

'I'm sure it'll be alright.' I take his hand and start pulling him towards the secluded glade.

'Christina! What's got into you?'

I roll my eyes and decide this is no time for being coy. With one hand placed firmly over Matt's crotch I look him square in the eye. 'We're alone Matt, and that kiss you gave me has turned me on. I want to go over into that glade and have sex with you under the Scottish sun.' Now his eyes are the ones going wide. 'You said you were up for trying new things. This just might be the way you get me screaming and digging my nails into your back.'

The lad doesn't need telling twice.

Within moments, we're in the glade and lying down on a bed of soft, dry grass, kissing and fumbling with each other's zippers. Matt pulls my combat trousers off in such a manly way, I nearly start to salivate. I start to pull his jeans down, but he stops me with a firm hand.

'Not yet. Let me... let me do some stuff to you first.'

That either sounds sexy as hell, or deeply disconcerting, depending on your frame of mind. 'What kind of stuff?'

He blushes red, as is the norm when discussing new sexual opportunities. 'Well, I've been on the internet again...'

'Oh, good God.'

He waves a hand. 'Just, just trust me. This is something you'll like.'

'How do you know if I'm going to like it, before you even - *oh my!*'

Matt's head has disappeared between my legs.

I have never been much of a fan of the world wide web, to be honest. I've always found it to be a bit too complicated for my liking, and all that social media rubbish passes me by completely. As far as I've been able to make out, the internet is full of useless information, horrible people hiding behind fake identities, and has done far more harm than good when it comes to meaningful human interaction.

Over the next few minutes though, I am forced to totally reconsider my position.

I now firmly believe the internet to be THE GREATEST INVENTION IN HUMAN HISTORY.

My head falls back against the soft warm bed of grass as Matt continues to dot com the hell out of my clitoris.

This is a *stupendously* excellent way to spend a late Sunday morning.

Above my head, I see striking blue skies ringed by branches of proud, strong pine trees. A few wisps of cloud float across the azure expanse, and a gentle breeze caresses my face.

This.

Is.

Fucking.

Bliss.

My eyes close as Matt changes tempo slightly with his tongue, to send me riding off on a fresh wave of pleasure. I clamp my legs around his head as my brain starts to rocket skyward to join the clouds.

With a gasp, my eyes fly open again, expecting to see the blue sky above me, the perfect visual accompaniment to my oncoming orgasm.

There is no blue sky though.

There is only portly Beagle head.

The chubby dog is looking down at me quizzically, his long snout nearly touching my forehead.

I am transfixed with immediate horror.

The Beagle, who - as a dog - thinks nothing of having sex in front of others, is obviously unaware of my immediate distress, and gives me a friendly lick on the nose. He then makes a deep huffing noise and licks me again, this time right across my left eye.

'Matt!' I screech, scaring the dog away.

Bunion looks up from his administrations. 'What's the matter? Am I doing something wrong?'

I don't have time to explain. I just push his head away from my vagina, and go scrabbling for my combat trousers.

Matt looks forlorn. 'Shit. I'm sorry! I thought I was doing it right, but I must not have read the web page correc - *oh Jesus Christ, there's a fucking dog watching us.*'

'Yes, there is Matt!' I wail, yanking on the combats. 'He belongs to that old couple. They must be over there too!'

The Beagle is now regarding us with curiosity from a safe distance. His head is cocked to one side.

'Shoo!' Matt cries and flaps his hands in the dog's direction. The Beagle ignores this, of course. He's a dog, not a small budgerigar.

I get my Caterpillars on in short order and am on my feet again, head whipping around, looking for signs of the dog's owners.

'We should get back to the path,' Matt suggests.

'Yes. We should,' I reply in a rather strained voice.

The Beagle, finally convinced the show is over, makes off back towards the path. We follow, hoping and praying that his owners are still far enough down the path that they don't see us as we reappear from the woods.

Nope.

There they are, right in bloody front of us.

'Good morning to you,' the old boy says in a thick Highland accent.

'Morning!' Matt and I say together, a little too quickly.

'Sorry if wee Bonneville scared you,' the woman says. 'He's a nosy old fool sometimes.'

'Oh, no trouble,' Matt tells her. 'We were just... we were just...'

Great, his mind's frozen. I'll have to come up with an excuse. 'We were just examining some interesting moss formations,' I hurriedly interject.

The old woman's eyebrow shoots up. 'Were you now?'

'Yes.'

'I see. Well, some of the moss appears to have gotten into your hair there, lass.' She points at my head. 'You must've been examining it *very, very* closely.'

I reach up and pull the small thatch of moss out of my hair, issuing a smile of ingratiating stupidity as I do so.

'I think we should be getting back to the hotel,' Matt says, all in one breath. 'It was nice to meet you both!' He looks down at the Beagle and gives him the stink eye. 'And you too Bonneville.'

The dog replies with another deep huff, before trotting back into the undergrowth.

'Nice to meet you too,' the old man says.

His wife smiles knowingly. 'Good luck with your moss investigations,' she says, evidently trying to suppress a chuckle.

'I think we got away with it,' Matt says as we tramp back down the hill.

'Only if they were both brain damaged. They knew what we were up to.'

Matt's face twists. 'Eww. But they were *old*.'

'Yes, but once upon a time, before Bonneville the Beagle, they were *young*. If she believed we were looking for moss, then I'm Billy Connolly.'

'I can't believe that dog found us like that.'

I let out a sigh that speaks volumes. 'I can. We seem to suffer from a severe case of *coitus interruptus* on a frighteningly regular basis.'

'Hmm,' he says thoughtfully. 'Maybe that's why you've developed your little problem. Something always pops up before your eyeballs roll back into your head.'

I let out a derisory snort. 'I wish. Trust me, there have been times when I wished for something to come along and interrupt proceedings before I either fell asleep, or had to go to the hospital for friction burns.' I catch sight of Matt's forlorn expression. 'Not with *you.*'

'Well, we'll just have to keep trying until we succeed!' he exclaims, pointing one purposeful finger skyward.

Bless him, I know he's only trying to help, but this may end up putting unnecessary pressure on me, which isn't exactly the right frame of mind you want when you're trying to have sex that ends with a proper climax. I'm willing to keep supporting Matt's crusade (after all, I have a great deal to gain if he's successful) but if it reaches the point where it starts to cloud our relationship, I'll have to take steps...

Our final day in Scotland is something of a wash-out, given the fact that even unseasonably warm weather doesn't hang around for long in the Scottish Highlands, before getting bullied out of the way by gusts of forty mile an hour wind, and cold, stinging rainfall. We spend the day reading books and taking advantage of the free wi-fi. I also take the chance to spend another hour in the sauna, followed by an equal amount of indulgent time in the jacuzzi.

All good things must come to an end though, and by 5pm we're driving back towards Glasgow, and I'm already mourning the salted caramel and chocolate pudding. I look for some in the airport - it gives me something to do in the three hours we have to wait before our flight takes off. I am wholly unsuccessful, you'll be amazed to learn. The nearest I can get would be to melt a Mars Bar over a Cadbury's Caramel and a pile of salt with a butane lighter - which really wouldn't be quite the same thing, I'm sure.

The 8pm flight is sparsely occupied. This is no bad thing, as even on short flights, it's always nice to know you won't be breathing in the farts of lots of other people. There is also less likelihood of catching a skin disease or the flu. Matt and I find ourselves right at the back of the plane, where we have at least four rows in front of us entirely empty.

We've been in the air for less than twenty minutes when Matt leans over and suggests we join the Mile High club.

'What?' I respond in mild disbelief.

'It's quiet. The toilets are just behind us...'

'Oh well, you are Captain Romantic, aren't you?'

'I just thought it might be sexy. Lots of people do it. I read it on the internet.'

'Rich people Matt. On private charter planes. On flights that last for hours. We're on an hour long public flight, on a plane owned by a budget airline. It sounds about as erotic as drinking a pint of Cillit Bang.'

He shrugs his shoulders. 'Okay... just an idea. Don't worry about it.'

Matt returns to reading the in-fight magazine with a slight sigh.

But now he's put the bloody idea in my head, hasn't he?

I contemplate the notion for a few minutes, watching for any signs of movement ahead of us. There isn't much. The few other passengers that are on the flight are either sleeping, on their iPads, or staring out of the window.

'Alright, come on then,' I half whisper. 'Let's give it a shot.'

'Really?' The look of cosmic delight on his face is quite something to behold.

'Yes. What we did in the forest yesterday was hot as hell... until Bonneville showed up anyway. Maybe I've got a thing for sex in public places.'

'Blimey. Right then.' Matt actually looks a little shocked - despite the fact that this was his idea. 'Really?' he repeats, staring at me quizzically.

What is it with men sometimes? It's perfectly natural and normal for them to be the ones acting all adventurous and a bit dirty, but if a woman feels the same way, they get uncomfortable.

I grab his hand and haul us both to our feet, my eyes locked on the front of the cabin. There is still no-one watching us.

Backing up the aisle like two secret agents hiding from the enemy, we make our way to the toilet door. I open it as quietly as possible, and we both sneak inside, locking the door behind us carefully.

The toilet is unsurprisingly tiny. So much so that our noses are almost touching.

'So how do we do this?' Matt asks.

'I don't know. This was your idea. Didn't you see anything on the internet?'

'Not about the specifics like this, no.'

I sniff. 'In case you haven't noticed, it does smell of poo in here.'

'Try to ignore it.'

'Okay...'

Now, I don't know about you, but trying to ignore the smell of poo is not something I want to be doing when contemplating sexual shenanigans. But we're here now, so I'll try to make the best of it.

'Maybe if I turn around and lean against the sink?' I suggest.

'Yeah, yeah, let's try that.'

I oblige by shuffling round an awkward one hundred and eighty degrees, and unzip my jeans. From behind me, I can here Matt fumbling about. I look into the rather tiny mirror in front of me to see him looking down, his penis held in one hand. He is thrusting his hips forward in an awkward jerking motion. 'You're not going to get very far doing that out there, you know,' I point out.

He shakes his head and looks over his shoulder. 'My belt has got caught on the little coat hook thing. I can't get it off.' He thrusts his hips forward again, looking like he's presenting me with his penis in some kind of prehistoric mating ritual. It stabs me in the bottom a couple of times, which is *incredibly* sexy, as I'm sure you can imagine.

Eventually Matt frees himself and pulls his jeans and boxers down, ready to do the deed. I try to part my legs a little, but can't do it much, as the toilet bowl is against one leg, and the door is against the other.

This is rather like trying to have sex in a plastic coffin.

Nevertheless, Matt's penis is still happy about the whole thing and he attempts to slide it into me, in order to get the ball rolling on this sexual experiment at 30,000 feet.

Here's the thing though, staring down at a small steel sink, a soap dispenser, and a disposal unit for sanitary towels is not something that makes Christina Barclay rampantly horny. 'Matt... Matt... MATT!'

'What?'

'Stop trying. You're more likely to get it in the captain's ear hole right now than my vagina.'

'What's wrong?'

Pulling up my jeans, I shuffle back around so I'm facing him again, and put one hand on his shoulder. 'Let's just say the fantasy of the Mile High Club is so much better than the reality - unless you're into sanitary towel dispensers.'

Matt makes a face that suggests he's conjured up a mental image that he'd rather not have. This puts paid to any erection he may have been harbouring in case I had a change of heart.

What makes the failure of this particular attempt at danger sex complete, is that when I open the toilet door again, there is a middle-aged woman standing there, with a poorly concealed look of impatience on her face. Impatience turns to incredulity as Matt sheepishly follows me out of the toilet, along with the faint whiff of poo that had partially put me off the whole idea in the first place. Christ knows what she must think: *There's obviously been some sex going on, but the smell of poo as well? What kind of disgusting animals are these two?*

I open my mouth to give voice to an apology, but there really is no point. The plane will be landing in a few minutes, so I won't have to be around the woman for long - sparing me much embarrassment.

Matt obviously feels differently. 'Sorry,' he says, as he passes her by. 'I was having a bit of trouble, so my girlfriend came in to help me out.'

As explanations go, this is absolutely *terrible*. The middle-aged woman is already convinced that we are two sexual perverts with a poo fetish, but now she gets to ruminate on exactly what 'help me out' could possibly mean.

I try not to look at Matt as the plane comes in to land. If I do, there's every chance I'll strangle him with the oxygen mask.

TWO'S COMPANY, THREE'S AN ARGUMENT

So we come to Matt Bunion's final attempt at injecting something kinky into our sex life that might result in me achieving an orgasm for the first time in his company. Without a shadow of a doubt, he's saved the best for last.

And the *worst*.

It's a week before my thirtieth birthday, and I am therefore incredibly grumpy. Anyone who says they are looking forward to turning thirty is a complete liar, and should not be trusted as far as you can throw them. Thirty represents the start of the horrifying slide from youth into middle-age... and don't let anyone tell you different.

To compound my grumpiness, I've just done ten days at work straight, thanks to stupidly agreeing to take on extra shifts at the beginning of the year. My bank account may approve, but my general state of well-being most definitely does not. Ten days as an inner city A&E nurse is rather like being placed into a tumble dryer on constant spin, while somebody throws morons at you.

In the last week and a half I have stitched up so many drunk idiots, it's a wonder I'm not over the legal limit myself, just from fume inhalation. And judging from the never-ending stream of people coming through the doors who have injured themselves at home in one stupid way or another, it's a wonder the human race has survived for as long as it has. It shouldn't be possible to injure yourself with a small biscuit tin or a Sky Plus remote control, but by crikey, some people have a bloody good go at it.

'A Sky Plus remote?' Matt asks as he takes a bite of his pizza.

'Yep,' I reply in a flat tone and sip my vodka and coke. I don't normally drink hard spirits these days if I can help it, but on a Friday night in the local Prezzo after ten days of hospital hell, nothing else will do the job.

'How?'

'Well, if you drop a plastic remote control on a polished hardwood lounge floor, and are too lazy to pick it up, don't be surprised when your evening is ruined an hour later, when you walk across the room to go for a pee, having forgotten where you left it.'

'Ouch. Nasty injury?'

'Yep. Tearing your anterior cruciate ligament when you're a professional footballer is a hazard of the job - doing it when you're *watching* professional football is just plain stupid.'

'You sound like you've had it up to here with patients.'

'You could say that,' I reply, and poke an angry fork into my linguini.

Matt then changes the subject completely, which is probably just as well, otherwise I'd be likely to launch into a pasta spitting tirade about drunks, idiots, drunk idiots, my new shift pattern, and the whole management structure of the NHS. 'You still coming over tomorrow night?' he inquires.

Bugger. I'd forgotten about that. While I'd probably prefer a night of Gerard Butler and fluffy dressing gowns, I had promised to spend the evening round Matt's watching a movie. This job can put a dampener on your love life, if you let it.

Matt sees the expression I'm making. 'Trust me, it'll be worth your while!'

'Why?' I ask suspiciously. Bunion has a habit of pulling surprise rabbits out of the hat (literally in one testicle swelling instance) and it sounds like there's another homing into view.

His conspiratorial smile and waggle of the eyebrows confirms it. 'You'll see. Just be round mine at seven thirty.'

'Matt, I'm not sure if I can take another sexy surprise right now. I've had a bad week.'

'Like I say, trust me. This will be different.' A twinkle has appeared in his eye. 'This is one thing I guarantee will excite the hell out of you.'

Okay, despite myself I'm curious again. The bondage gear and plane toilet may have both been mistakes, but I'm a firm believer in third time lucky... for some unfathomable reason. 'What have you got in store for me this time?'

The smile broadens. 'You'll see. Let's just say I hope you fancy a bit of dressing up.'

My curiosity withers. 'Dressing up?' I utter, my eyes narrowing. 'If you think I'm doing any kind of kinky nurse and sexy patient stuff, you've got another thing coming, boy.'

It wouldn't be the first time a man has tried that one on. Can you imagine how unsexy it is to have a man suggest bringing some kind of fetish version of your work clothes into the bedroom? The last thing I want to be reminded of when I'm in bed is bloody work.

Matt shakes his head. 'Oh come on, give me some credit here. I've got no interest in playing doctors and nurses with you. Especially not after the horror stories you've been telling me over the past few weeks. Being a nurse sounds about as erotic as being a bin man.'

'Thank God for that.'

'Don't worry. What I've got planned is *definitely* something you're going to find sexy...'

The twinkle is brighter than ever.

I don't know whether I should be excited, or worried about taking out an even better life insurance policy.

It is with some trepidation that I ring the bell on Matt's front door the next evening. He flings the door open a scant second after the bell has started playing the Imperial March. 'Evening Christina!' he exclaims happily. Clearly he has been eagerly awaiting my arrival.

'Evening,' I reply slowly. In the drive over here I have conjured up all sorts of private nightmares about what Matt has in store this evening. I have images of being stuffed into a leather Catwoman costume, while Matt prances around waving his Batarang at my boobs.

When men say they want to engage in a little sexy dress up, it usually means for their edification, not yours.

'Come in, come in!' he says, ushering me through the door and down the hallway to the lounge. I notice that Matt picks up a little speed as we pass the door to the spare room, hurrying me by it. There must be something in there he doesn't want me to see.

This is all *very* fishy...

Once in the lounge, Matt bids me sit down on the sofa. 'Shall we have a drink?' he asks. 'Red wine alright with you?'

'Yeah, okay,' I reply warily. 'I have a feeling I'm going to need it.'

'Ha ha! Matt laughs, a little too loudly. He pours me a glass of the red stuff, and himself a beer, and comes and sits next to me. 'So, how was your day?' he asks earnestly.

'Um... fine.'

'Excellent! Get up to anything interesting?' Matt leans forward attentively.

This is just getting weirder and weirder. 'You know what I did Matt. I went to see my parents.'

'Oh yes! And how are they? Is your mother better from her cold? You said it had gone to her chest. It sounds horrible. How is she?'

'Look, what the bloody hell are you up to?'

'What do you mean?'

'You've never met my mother. Why are you so concerned with her state of health?'

'Just showing a little interest in my girlfriend's life,' Matt pouts.

'Rubbish, you're up to something. Spill it.'

Matt stands up suddenly. 'Oh alright. I'm trying to make you feel comfortable.'

'Comfortable?'

'Yes. The article I read online said that before introducing a new and different sexual experience, you should make a woman feel at ease. It suggests that engaging her in conversation about her day would be a good way to do it.'

'Really? Let me guess, this article was written by a man, wasn't it?'

'Might've been,' Matt mumbles.

'Thought so.' I put my wine glass down and exhale deeply. 'Why don't we just get down to what all this is about? I don't think I can take a round of twenty questions about how much phlegm my mother is still producing.'

'But you have to feel comfortable.'

'I'll be a lot more comfortable if we don't mention my parents again, Matt. Just get on with whatever it is you've been planning, eh? Didn't you say something about dressing up? A bit of role play?'

'I did!'

'Great. Why not break out the Catwoman costume then, so we can get on with it.'

'What?'

'I assume that's what you've got for me to wear? Or maybe Princess Leia's gold bikini?'

Matt looks hurt. 'I'm not that bad.'

'Really? Are you trying to tell me you haven't thought about dressing me up as one of your fantasy female characters?'

'No!' He squints thoughtfully. 'Well, *yes*. Of course I have. But not tonight. Tonight's all about *your* fantasy.'

'Is it?'

'Yeah! And to start it, you need to go into the bedroom. There's something waiting for you in there. I've turned the heating up, so you won't be cold... and nor will I for that matter.'

'Are we going to have sex dressed as lizards?'

'Very funny. Just go into the bedroom and put on what you find in there.'

I drain the rest of my wine and get off the couch. 'Okay. I'll play along.' I point a cautionary finger at him. 'But if this ends in a trip to casualty again, don't blame me.'

'It won't, I promise. Just put on the outfit lying on the bed, and I'll be in shortly.'

'Are you dressing up too?'

He rocks his hand back and forth. 'Sort of. It's more dressing down to be honest.'

I raise an eyebrow, but say no more. This is sounding stranger and stranger by the minute, but what have I got to lose? After all, we're in private and alone, so whatever transpires will just be between the two of us. How bad can it be?

Inside Matt's steamy bedroom I find out what he wants me to wear. It's a toga. Like something straight out of a Roman epic, it's small, made of white, diaphanous material, and will barely cover my modesty. No wonder Matt turned the heating up.

I hold the toga up and a smile creases my lips.

This actually isn't that bad.

I wouldn't pop into John Lewis to pick up a new wok wearing it, but for some bedroom fun it certainly fits the bill.

I'm a girl who's used to wearing jeans and a t-shirt whenever I can get away with it, so I'm not used to having soft, floating material against my body. It's quite the experience, let me tell you. It *shifts* and *moves* over your skin in an extremely pleasant manner.

Matt, perhaps predicting that I'd like the outfit, has propped a full length mirror against one of his bedroom walls, which I now take full advantage of. I have to say I like what I see. Well, more or less anyway. I still think my thighs are a bit too large, I'd like to be a cup size larger, and my arms look a tiny bit flabby, but on the whole, I think I wear the toga rather well.

I spend a good five minutes admiring myself, before Matt knocks politely on the door. This is as good an indication of the kind of guy he is as you're likely to get. He knocks on his own bedroom door instead of just coming straight in. 'How are you doing?' I hear his muffled voice say.

'I'm wearing it!'

'Do you like it?'

'Actually Matt, I do. It's a lot better than what I was expecting!'

'Good.' There's a brief pause. 'Can I take it that you're standing by the mirror then?'

I blush. Preening in front of a full length mirror is okay when nobody else knows you're doing it, but the idea that somebody else knows you're a colossal narcissist is rather troubling. 'I was just having a little look, yes,' I reply quickly.

'Thought so! Can you go and lie on the bed please?'

'Do we have to conduct this conversation through the door? Why don't you just come in?'

'I don't want to ruin the surprise! Just go and lie down.'

I do as Matt asks and stretch myself out. 'Right, I'm here.'

'Great. Under the pillow on the left side is a red silk blindfold. Can you put it on?'

I feel around, and sure enough, there is a soft, long blindfold underneath the pillow. 'I'm not sure about this,' I tell him. 'Are you going to wave a portly beagle in my face when I take it off?'

'Very funny. Just go along with it please?'

Smiling despite myself, I tie the blindfold around my head and my world goes black. 'I'm ready.'

'You can't see anything?'

'Nope. Completely in the dark.'

'Cool. I'm coming in then.'

The door opens and I hear Matt walk into the room. I say walk, I mean clank. There's definitely some kind of armour involved in whatever outfit he's chosen to wear for my amusement. While I can't see him, the room is small enough for me to sense that he passes by me on the bed and goes to stand at the end of it.

'Okay, you can take the blindfold off now,' Matt says, his voice a little squeaky.

With a swift movement I pull the silky material from my eyes and behold what Bunion has wrought.

Oh lord...

Oh good lord above...

Matt is naked, save a red cloak, a red pleather codpiece, a pointy helmet with a faceplate, and high Grecian style sandals. He is also carrying a spear and shield, both of which are quite clearly plastic. In other words, he's come dressed as Gerard Butler from *300* - the fancy dress shop equivalent anyway. All that's missing is the beard.

...and possibly the washboard stomach.

...and the huge arm muscles.

...and the glistening thighs.

Apart from all *that* though, I have my own King Leonidas to play with this evening.

Matt clears his throat. 'This is Sparta?' he says in a strangled voice, and waves his spear about a bit. He then coughs. 'Let me try that again... THIS IS SPARTA!' he roars as loudly as his larynx will allow, and holds both shield and spear aloft.

My hands fly to my mouth, partly in shock, and partly to prevent a loud bray of laughter erupting from between my lips.

'What do you think?' he asks, in the most uncertain voice I've ever heard.

'Oh Matt... oh, oh Matt.' I'm struggling to get the words out. I'm so close to losing it that if I try to speak, I'm likely to cackle with laughter at the top of my lungs.

His shoulders slump. 'You think it's stupid, don't you?'

Get it together girl. He's gone to a lot of effort here for you.

I swallow down the traitorous bubble of hilarity, and rise to my knees, scuttling across the bed towards Matt with my arms wide. 'No. I don't think it's stupid. I think you're a lovely man,' I say and put my arms around him.

He hangs his head. 'It's just that you said how much you loved Gerard Butler in *300*, so I thought I'd... I'd...'

'Recreate it with you as the King and me as his Queen?' I finish for him.

Matt nods. 'Yeah, that was the idea.'

'And it's a great idea,' I reassure him and run one hand down the front of my outfit seductively. 'This toga is making me feel very sexy.' I place my other hand on his red pleather codpiece. 'Now, why don't we lie down and you can see how long it takes you to get it off me?' I pause to look up at Matt's Spartan paraphernalia. 'But take the helmet off and leave the weaponry on the floor, eh?'

The helmet flies off and clonks Howard The Duck on the head, while the shield and spear drop to the floor with a clatter. 'And the cloak,' I add. 'It makes you look a bit like Superman.' The red cloak is untied as well, before Matt grabs me around the waist and pulls me down onto the bed.

Now he's divested himself of the sillier aspects of his costume, I can certainly appreciate the rest of it. While Matt is not built like Mr Butler, he is tall, with a decent set of shoulders, and a physique that you could easily describe as fit, if a little skinny. He could do with two weeks in the sun and a few more in the gym, but overall he's more than enough to get this girl's engine revving.

I straddle Matt's waist and start to kiss him passionately. The red codpiece is thin enough for me to instantly tell that he's very happy about this.

'I know I'm not quite like the guy in the movie,' he says between kisses.

'You're fine!' I reply and kiss him again.

Matt holds me by the shoulders and pulls me away. 'I know, but I also know how much you like the men in that movie.'

'Don't worry about it! You're more than sexy enough for me in this outfit, Matt!' I try to kiss him again, but he holds me back.

Just what the hell is going on?

'There's one more thing I've arranged,' he tells me, and moves out from under my body.

'What?' I snap rather impatiently. I'm done with the costumed foreplay now, I just want to get to the main event!

Matt goes and stands by the stereo resting on his chest of drawers. 'Sit back on the bed Christina. You're going to get the full *300* effect tonight!' He grins, and flicks the machine on. Loud, percussive electronic music starts to blare out of the speakers. It's the theme tune from the movie.

'What the hell are you doing?!' I shout at Matt over the din.

'Just watch!' he roars.

Suddenly, the bedroom door flies open with a loud crash. I scream in surprise and horror and whip my head around to see Gerard Butler storm into the room. He's wearing his *300* gear and looks *magnificent*. The beard is long and flowing, the muscles are tanned and glistening, the stomach is so washboard like I'm tempted to run home and get my smalls, just so I can soap them up and run them across his abs.

It's *unbelievable*! Matt has actually paid the Hollywood movie star to come to his flat tonight and perform for me -

Hang on! That isn't Gerard Butler!

He's too short for starters - by a good five inches, it appears. And he's slightly balding. Gerard Butler isn't five foot seven and thinning on top - not unless the movie make-up artists are even better at their jobs than I thought.

Other than these obvious differences though, the Butler lookalike is quite convincing.

Right up to the point he starts to thrust his pelvis in my face and lick his lips at me. In all my sexual fantasies involving the star of *300*, I have never once pictured him gyrating his hips like that, or giving me a look of such sexual aggression that it makes my vagina want to curl up and die.

I look over at Matt in horror. He returns my stunned gaze with a look of excited encouragement. I turn back to the Butler lookalike to see that he has removed his own cloak and is now facing away from me, rubbing both hands over his stacked buttocks. Said buttocks are also rotating in a manner that is almost hypnotic. Before they can lull me into a coma, I turn back to Matt once again. 'What the hell is this?!' I scream over the pounding music, pointing at the gyrating madman.

'Sexy, eh? It's like he's right out of the movie!'

Butler's doppelganger has ceased rubbing his buttocks, and is now facing me again, grabbing at his crotch and licking his lips once more. If there were any sex offenders running around Greece two thousand years ago, this is exactly what they would have looked like.

'Who is this person?!' I screech at Matt.

Matt gives me a thumbs up. 'He's for you, baby! I know I don't look like Gerard Butler, so I hired somebody that does!'

'Hired somebody?!'

'Yeah, he's from a male escort service! They specialise in costumed fantasies!'

***

I'm gobsmacked. Matt has rented a muscular male prostitute to come here and dance for me. 'And you thought I'd like that?!' I shout, even louder now that the music is reaching a crescendo.

'Yeah, of course! I paid for the full package, so you can do anything you like with him!'

My lip curls in disgust. 'What do you mean by *do anything I like with him*?!'

Matt shrugs his shoulders. 'Well, he is a male escort!'

This just gets worse and worse.

'Oh, so fake Gerard isn't just here to dance for me. I can *fuck* him too if I like?!'

'If you want. I got the idea for getting an escort from this website I saw!'

'A website?! What was it called Matt?'

'Can't 'member,' he mumbles.

'What was it called?!'

'Ma' 'er 'um 'arder dot 'om.'

'What?!'

'Make her cum harder dot com.'

I clench both fists. 'You are unbelievable! You're getting sexual advice from a fucking *porn site*? In what universe did you think I would want to have sex with - *oh good god, he's got his cock out!*'

Not only has fake Gerard pulled his sizeable penis out from the pleather codpiece, he is now swinging it around in a circular motion. I believe this is called 'doing the helicopter'.

That's it. I've had enough.

I leap from the bed, push Matt out of the way and flick off the terrible din emanating from the speakers. Gerard continues to helicopter his willy around for a few moments before realising the music has finished. As it flops back between his legs he leers and me. 'Oh, we done wit' the dancin' then?' he says in the broadest Lancashire accent I've ever heard. 'You want to get down t' some of the 'orny stuff, do yer?' Lancashire's finest Spartan warrior gently thrusts his penis at me, underlining his question.

At first, there are no words. No words to respond with. I have simply never found myself in such a ludicrous situation before. I'm in a bedroom roughly the same temperature as the surface of the sun, with two men dressed as Spartan warriors, one of whom has his unfeasibly large Lancashire sausage pointed in my general direction. The other man is staring at me in a combination of shock and dread. I assume this is because he knows what's coming.

'Get out,' I hiss at fake Gerard.

His brow creases. 'But yer boyfriend here paid for the full monty. You don't want it, luv?

'No Gerard, I do not fucking *want it.*'

'Me name's not Gerard, it's Barry.'

'Barry then! Get out Barry! Get out now!'

Matt steps between us, sensing imminent violence. 'Er, I think you'd better do as she says Barry. Just grab your clothes from the spare room and go.'

Barry's brow furrows even more. 'You don't get no refund, you know that, don't yer?'

'Yes, yes, that's fine. Just leave!' Matt replies in a desperate voice.

Barry - still with penis dangling, I might add - picks up his Spartan cloak and leaves the room without another word, closing the door behind him as he goes. This will be the easiest job he's ever had as a male escort, I'm sure. There aren't many occasions in that line of work when you can get away with just a bit of cockcopter before being finished for the night.

Matt turns back around to face my righteous fury.

'Just what did you think you were doing Matt?!' I spit at him.

'I just thought... I just thought... '

'You just thought I would be up for a threesome with you and the Northern Cock Warrior, did you?'

'It wasn't like that! He was meant for you!'

'And that's the kind of woman you think I am, is it? One who'll shag any old Barry just because he's built like a brick shithouse?'

Matt's mouth turns down at both corners and his arms hang loose by his side. He is the very picture of dejection. 'But it's *300*. You like that film.'

'I also quite liked Toy Story. Are Woody and Buzz about to burst through the door and wave their penises at me?'

I deeply apologise for the hideous mental image that no doubt conjures up. Nobody needs to think of beloved children's characters indecently exposing themselves, but I'm angry right now and don't have much control over what I'm saying.

'Don't be silly.'

'I'm not the one being silly, Matt! I didn't invite a complete stranger into our sex lives!'

'I'm leavin' now!' Barry cries from over by the front door.

'Yes, yes! Just go!' Matt responds.

'Both sure yer don't want the full service? Only, I bought the baby oil and me largest dil - '

'Fuck off Barry!' I rage.

He doesn't need telling twice. I hear the front door slam as I start to pull off the toga and go for my street clothes.

'What are you doing?' Matt asks with a defeated whine in his voice.

'Leaving Matt. I feel the need to be away from you for a while.'

'Please don't be angry with me. I was just trying to help you feel sexy...'

Oh, that's unfair. Here I am in full on rage mode and Bunion is giving it the sad puppy dog eyes. It's quite distracting. If I stay around any longer I'll end up feeling sorry for him, and that just won't do. I understand that he was trying to do something nice for me, but to try to get me to fuck another bloke is such a blunder of epic proportions that it deserves a little time in the dog house. 'I am going home Matt,' I tell him as I finish dressing.

His mouth opens. He's about to argue. Then he catches the flintiness of my expression and decides against it. 'Okay. Will I see you again? It's your birthday next week.'

Of course he will. This evening has been a disaster, but it's the only real disaster so far, so I don't see any reason to break the relationship off.

Matt doesn't need to know that though. 'I'm not sure. I guess I'll have to think about it,' I tell him.

Something twists in my heart as I watch his face crumple, but I must remain resolute. I picture Barry grasping at his crotch and leering at me, which strengthens my resolve.

I pick up the toga and stride past Matt, opening the front door myself. Mercifully there is no sign of Barry now.

'Bye Christina. Er... drive safe,' Matt tells me as I exit the flat. He looks a little pathetic standing there in his red pleather codpiece.

'Go back inside. You'll catch your death,' I advise him, before marching off down the garden path, one eye twitching as I go.

When I get home the first thing I do is find my DVD of *300* and throw it in the bin. There's no way I can ever watch it again. When the opening credits start to roll I'll just picture Lancashire Barry's wildly flailing penis, and the whole thing will be ruined.

The second thing I do is give the toga a quick iron and hang it up in the wardrobe. It might come in handy in the future. I may not be a woman so adventurous that she wants to take on two men in pleather codpieces, but that doesn't mean I'm one to look a gift horse in the mouth.

Thinking of the word horse just reminds me of Barry again, so I have to go for a long lie down in the dark.

K.I.S.S

My birthday dawns bright and clear.

This is the first time it's fallen on Easter Sunday for as long as I can remember, but you couldn't have nicer weather for both occasions.

Sadly, I'm not really in much of a fit state to enjoy it as I'm righteously hung over, thanks to a night out with the girls from work. I fell through the door at 3am. It's now 11am, and I *think* I'm sober again - but I wouldn't want to bet my driving licence on it.

When one is in a delicate state such as this, quiet serenity is most definitely the order of the day. Hence the fact I'm now sat out in the sunny back garden with a nice cup of tea and two Nurofen working their way through my bloodstream.

My dreamy haze is rudely interrupted by my mobile phone going off. Hilariously, the girls must have gotten hold of the phone last night while I was drunk off my arse, and downloaded a Justin Bieber song to use as my ringtone. The cheeky cows have also turned the volume up full. The peace and calm of my hung over Sunday morning is shattered by the Canadian spunk trumpet wailing '*Baby, Baby, Baby, Ohhhhh!*' at the top of his girlish lungs. I answer the call as swiftly as possible just to shut him up.

'Hello?' I say irritably.

'Um... hi Christina.' Matt sounds very unsure of himself. I doubt the waspishness of my tone is helping.

'Morning Matt,' I say, wincing as my head throbs thanks to Justin's caterwauling.

'I just wanted to ring and say happy birthday.'

This is the first time we've spoken since the Night of Barry. I've been meaning to call him, but work and birthday preparations have taken up all of my time. I would feel bad about it, but this bloody headache won't let me.

'Thanks Matt.' I rub my eyes. 'It's nice to hear from you.'

'Is it?' He sounds amazed.

'Yes. It is. I'm sorry I haven't called.'

'That's okay. I kinda thought you were done with me after the other night. I've been thinking long and hard about it, and it really was a stupid plan, wasn't it?'

'Yep.'

'Anyway,' he says, changing the subject for all he's worth, 'as it's your birthday, I was wondering if I could come over and see you?'

I have to confess, for a moment I consider saying no. Not because I'm still angry at Matt, but because I feel like death warmed up. However, I have left the poor lad hanging for longer than I should have... and I would like to see him.

'Sure, come over about seven?'

'Sounds great!'

'And Matt?'

'You haven't been looking at anymore stuff on the internet, have you? I don't think I could take it.'

'No. I'm done with that.'

'You sure? Because I don't want to do anal, have no desire to dress you in a nappy, and my nipples are already way too sensitive to have anything clamped to them.'

This actually makes him laugh. It's a nice sound to hear in the bright morning sunlight. 'Nope. It'll just be me tonight. No silly surprises.'

'Great. See you later.'

I put the phone down and sit back in the chair, closing my eyes to let the sun warm them. Five minutes later I have to go inside, as the last vestiges of the alcohol in my system don't like direct sunlight and are dangerously close to making me throw up.

I hope to God I'll feel a bit better by the time Matt arrives. I want to restore some of the good feeling between the two of us, and me vomiting all over his shoes will *not* be the way to do it.

Luckily, I am feeling worlds better by seven o'clock. An hour long bath and several more Nurofen have taken the edge off the hangover nicely, and by the time the doorbell rings I am more or less back to my usual self.

Inexplicably, by mid afternoon I start to become a bit nervous about seeing Matt. I haven't felt like this at any stage previously in our whirlwind four month relationship, so I find it quite perplexing as to why I should be feeling it now.

Then it hits me - I'm *thirty*.

While I was in my twenties, I had no reason to feel older than Matt, but now I am a wizened old harridan - past my prime and no longer young, carefree or attractive in the slightest. He is still well in his twenties, so it's almost a guarantee that the second a woman not as crone-like as me homes into view, I'll be unceremoniously dumped and forced to fend for myself as I slip into old age.

Okay, I'm exaggerating wildly, but that psychological hang-up of entering my fourth decade on the planet is at the forefront of my mind as I choose an outfit to wear for Matt's arrival. I go with the nice light, floaty white dress, as I'm slightly worried anything tighter might set off the headache again. It also shows off my cleavage quite nicely, which appears to have survived the transition into my thirties without dropping six inches.

A very strange sight greets me when I open the front door to a rather timid knock. Usually, Mr Bunion is dressed in a pair of faded jeans, trainers, and a t-shirt depicting one sci-fi movie or another. I'm considerably shorter than he is, so there have been many times when I've gone in for a hug, only to be bogged out by C3PO or Godzilla. Today though, he is almost unrecognisable.

The wild hair has been wrestled into a degree of neatness, the Star Wars tee has been replaced with a smart dark red shirt, the jeans are brand new and clean, and instead of ratty Nike trainers, we have a polished pair of black shoes. Matt actually looks... like an adult!

A very handsome adult at that.

'Wow. You look very smart,' I tell him as he hovers on the doorstep, holding a carrier bag in front of him like it's a security blanket.

'Thanks Christina. You look beautiful.'

Well there you go... the cleavage dress must've been a good idea.

'Come in,' I say and let him in through the door. He shuffles in nervously. 'Matt?'

'Yeah?'

'You look like you're going to the gallows. I'm not bothered about what happened with Barry anymore, honestly.'

'Okay,' he says and nods his head with relief. 'I'm really pleased you're not mad at me.' He thrusts out the carrier bag. 'I've bought you a present... presents actually.'

'That's very kind of you.'

Matt's eyes go wide. 'Almost forgot!' He leans forward and kisses me on the cheek. 'Happy birthday,' he says softly, making me go annoyingly gooey.

'Thank you,' I reply, in a voice that has far too much school girl embarrassment in it for my liking. 'Would you like a coffee?'

I hurry past Matt so he doesn't have to see how red I've gone, and we go into the kitchen. There, he hands me the carrier bag. Inside is a birthday card - which is romantic, but not gushing, I'm pleased to say. You can tell when a man's thought about which card to buy. When they just pick up the first one that looks appropriate, they tend to be full of the worst kind of cheesy sentimentality that just proves he didn't look inside before taking it to the till.

To celebrate the fact that Jesus rose from the grave the same day I was born - this year anyway - Matt has also included a large Green & Blacks Easter Egg. It's a dark chocolate one, which is my favourite, so Bunion gets two ticks for the birthday gifts so far.

He gets a third, fourth and fifth tick for the actual present though. It's a beautiful silver necklace, featuring a gorgeous teardrop shaped filigree pendant. I don't get the chance to wear much jewellery, so I don't know how he knew what style I'd like, but the necklace is absolutely *perfect*.

'Oh Matt, it's stunning.'

'You really think so?'

'Yes. Help me put it on?' I turn away from him and lift up my hair so he can clasp it round my neck. He does so. 'Thanks. Now would you like that cup of coffee*eeeeee*...'

The reason for the rather odd end to that last sentence? Matt has just kissed the back of my neck in the softest, most pleasurable way possible.

I turn back around and let him kiss me on the lips as well. This, if anything, is even better. In fact, within a minute or so, I'm so turned on that I've even forgotten about the fact that I'm now thirty. Which says quite a lot, doesn't it?

Matt has really stepped up his game tonight.

The clothes, the card, the presents, the soft kisses... it's almost like he's a different person. It's just not like him to be so -

Hang on a bloody minute!

I pull away. 'Have you been on the sodding internet again?'

'What?'

'The internet, Matt. The source of all your romantic ideas? Without which I would never have tried to have sex in a plastic box at 30,000 feet, or seen the Barrycock?'

Matt contrives to look innocent of the charges laid before him. 'No. I said I hadn't done that again.'

'Are you sure Matthew?' Breaking out the full Christian name is a sure sign I mean business.

'Well...'

'Oh for crying out loud!'

'No, no wait. Alright, I confess I may have been on a couple of relationship forums, but I think I've got it right this time.'

'How Matt? How have you got it right this time?'

'Because this time, I'm going to follow my heart, instead of my head. That's the advice I got on the forum. Keep it simple, stupid! No bullshit, no gimmicks. I just want to tell you... tell you one thing.'

'What, Matt? What are you trying to say?' Judging by how pale he's suddenly become, it doesn't sound like it's going to be good.

Matt clears his throat. 'I know this is a bit out of the blue, and I know we haven't been together that long... but I love you Christina. With all my heart.'

I am, needless to say, completely fucking taken aback by this.

Our relationship has largely been based on sex thus far, so to hear those three little words come out of Matt's mouth is very surprising.

Surprising, but also very *pleasing*, I'm delighted to say.

I've known this boy for just four months, but they've been four *great* months - by and large. Okay, the whole Barrycock incident was a low point, and my thigh still doesn't feel quite right after the acute cramp, but both of those things only came about because I've finally met a man who cares about *me*. Matt's silly plans to help me reach an orgasm may have gone awry, but his heart has constantly been in the right place throughout. He's made an effort to put a smile on my face each and every moment we've been together. Which is rather marvellous when you think about it.

I come to a sudden and blinding realisation.

'I... I love you too, Matt,' I tell him, my voice cracking.

'You do?'

I roll the lovely pendant between my fingers. 'Yes. Yes, I do.'

He actually looks surprised. 'Oh... good! Good stuff!' he clears his throat again and looks around the kitchen. 'Er... not entirely sure what to do now. Never really been in love before... not with someone who loves me too, anyway.' He scratches his ear. 'It's a bit weird, to be honest.'

'Oh, come here, you big idiot,' I say, and put my arms around him.

'Can I... can I kiss you again?' he asks.

'If you love me, you'd better had, before I start to think your heart's not really in it.'

Matt's eyes go wide, he takes a deep breath, and immediately plants his lips back on mine.

For reasons which should be obvious, this is the best kiss we've ever shared.

There are more kisses in the kitchen over the next few minutes, followed by even more in the hallway.

The kisses are then punctuated by the removal of outer clothing on the landing, and the removal of underwear on the bed.

Before I know it, I find myself having sex with a man who is in love with me. And it is *wonderful*.

Like Matt said, this time there are no gimmicks, no toys, no costumes, and definitely no third parties. Just me and the man I've fallen in love with. This is exactly the way it should be.

It's not long before Matt is reaching the point of no return.

I've been in this particular situation before of course - with a man deep inside me, about to orgasm. Prior to this moment though, it's always been the point at which I've been left tragically left behind to fend for myself.

But tonight, things are very different.

I am in love.

Probably for the first time.

The orgasm, when it comes, is powerful, long, and decidedly toe-curling.

It is also the easiest and most natural thing that's ever happened to me.

The End

About the author:

Nick Spalding is an author who, try as he might, can't seem to write anything serious. He's worked in the communications industry his entire life, mainly in media and marketing. As talking rubbish for a living can get tiresome (for anyone other than a politician), he thought he'd have a crack at writing comedy fiction - with an agreeable level of success so far, it has to be said. Nick lives in the South of England with his fiancée. He is approaching his forties with the kind of dread usually associated with a trip to the gallows, suffers from the occasional bout of insomnia, and still thinks Batman is cool.

You can find out more about Nick by following him on **Twitter** or by reading his blog **Spalding's Racket**.

29217358R00063

Printed in Great Britain
by Amazon